JOB FOR A
GUNFIGHTER

"I want this valley and I'll get it. You don't scare me, you or your gun or the rep you've built. There's plenty of gunslingers as fast as you and I'll bring them in, as many as I need."

Lang Stobaugh was rotten to the core. He'd hire killers to get control of the valley. He'd take over the small ranches, one by one.

He had to be stopped and there was only one man quick enough and sure enough to do it . . . a man named Damaron.

Damaron's Gun

WESLEY RAY

WILDSIDE PRESS

Chapter 1

THE TRAIL OF THE KILLER LED NORTH AND BLAIN Damaron followed it, out of Texas and through New Mexico, and over Raton Pass into Colorado. Trinidad, Pueblo. A lot of towns and a lot of miles, but Damaron held to it and he knew now that the end was near.

In the mountain town of Silver, he missed his man by only a couple of hours. Lacey had pulled out, they said, heading toward Candelaria down in the valley. So Damaron got back in the saddle and rode on. There was dust on his shoulders, black stubble on his flat cheeks. He had gone without sleep; he had not rested enough, and it was beginning to tell on him. But thinking of the thousand dollars that the job would pay made him feel better.

He knew that Lacey was aware he was being followed; that was why the killer had not stopped for long in one place. He was trying to make it to Wyoming, Damaron had heard. Claimed he had some friends in the Hole-in-the-Wall country.

Coming down from the mountains, he looked at the valley stretching out below him. It was long and green and fertile, the tall grass waving in the breeze and the noonday sun shining on the Candelaria River. It was seven years since Damaron had seen it, but he told himself that the only thing he wanted here was a man named Al Lacey.

In the middle of the valley was the town of Candelaria where he used to go for supplies. The old homeplace was over there to the west, a little ten-cow outfit that his dad had tried to build into something. The place held no interest for Damaron now and his straying gaze came back to the trail.

If Lacey didn't stop in Candelaria, neither would Damaron. He would stick to the trail until he caught up with his man and when he found him he'd kill him and that would be the end of it. Not that Lacey had done him any wrong. He would kill him because killing was Damaron's business.

He was in the hills now, riding through familiar country, and it did not please him. He wished that Lacey had gone in some other direction. It occurred to him that he might have to kill the man on the streets of Candelaria, and there were places he'd rather have it happen. Then he shrugged, telling himself it didn't make a hell of a lot of difference.

Trees dotted the hillside, cedar for the most part, but he kept his eyes on the trail and now he saw a rider coming toward him. It was a man on a dappled gray, a man who rode as though he was in no rush to get anywhere. Damaron watched him carefully because in this business you couldn't afford to take chances.

Now that he was closer Damaron saw something familiar about the rider. When they met he recognized him and they both reined in. With some of the tension gone from him, Damaron smiled, and said, "Hello, Mace."

Mace Lawson ran blunt fingers over his fleshy face. He was a man close to fifty, big of belly and wide across the seat of his pants. He stared searchingly at Damaron. "Know you, but I can't place you just yet."

"The first name's Blain."

Lawson sat up straighter in his saddle. "Well, I'll be damned. You're Jim Damaron's boy. Changed a heap since the last time I saw you."

"Reckon I have."

Lawson shifted his weight and sunlight touched the badge pinned to his shiny black vest. "Wrote you about Jim, figured you'd want to come home for the funeral, but I never did hear from you."

"It was two months before the letter caught up with me."

Lawson studied him and there were a lot of questions in the fat man's eyes. Before he could ask them, Damaron said, "Pass anybody heading toward town?"

"Didn't meet nobody," Lawson said, shoving his black Stetson to the back of his head. "But when I came by the Vail store, there was a horse out front that I'd never seen before."

"A blaze-faced bay?"

"That's right."

Damaron lifted his reins. "How far to this store?"

"About a mile straight on," Lawson said, eyeing him curiously. "I reckon it wasn't homesickness that brought you back here."

"You're right, Mace." Damaron was looking beyond the fat man, scanning the trail. "If I don't see you again, so long."

When he started to ride on, Lawson hesitated a moment, then turned his mount and fell in alongside. "I was going over to the Perry place," he said, "but it ain't important."

6

Damaron didn't answer. His eyes were on the trail and he was thinking again of Lacey, wondering if the killer thought he was far enough ahead that he didn't have to worry.

"What about this blaze-faced bay?" Lawson asked.

"Belongs to a man I'm looking for," Damaron told him. "Fella named Al Lacey."

"Friend of yours?"

Damaron shook his head. "He killed a man in Fort Worth, shot him in the back, then lit out."

"Sounds like a job for the law."

"The law can't do much," Damaron said. "The kid was killed in an alley and nobody saw it happen."

"Then how do you know it was this Lacey?"

"Because the kid lived long enough to tell his dad who it was. His dad's a saloonman and the local law wanted more than just his word for it."

"So the kid's dad sent for you," Lawson said, nudging his horse as Damaron's mount got ahead of him. When they were side by side once more, Lawson spoke again. "From the stories I've heard, I guess he sent for the right man."

"I'm making no bones about it," Damaron said without resentment. "I'm a gunman, trailing this Lacey because there's money in it if I kill him."

Lawson swallowed hard and was quiet for a time. Then he said heavily, "Your old daddy would turn over in his grave if he heard you talking that way."

Damaron didn't look at the fat man. "We never saw things alike."

As though he hadn't heard, Lawson said, "Jim Damaron was one of the finest men I ever knew."

Yeah, Damaron thought, and what had it got him? A few friends, maybe, and a wife who hadn't lived long after he brought her to this valley. Damaron remembered him, a man with white hair and a stern face who read the Good Book and was satisfied with a little piece of ground with a shack on it.

Jim Damaron had talked of peace and tried to set an example for his neighbors. He didn't wear a gun, claiming that men would never get along with one another until they learned to live without them. They hadn't learned, Damaron thought, and now Jim Damaron was dead and what had he accomplished while he lived?

He hadn't even been able to instill in his own son the things he believed in. Guns had held a fascination for Da-

7

maron at an early age. He remembered when he used to go over to the Perrys', their neighbors, and see the long-barreled Colt that hung over the mantle. He knew he wasn't supposed to fool with it, but he'd stand and look and one day when he was alone in the room he had taken the gun down and held it in his hand. . . .

Bringing his mind back to the present, he said, "This store you mentioned wasn't here when I left."

"No, a fella built it couple of years ago. Saves some of the ranchers a trip to town."

They were close to the Candelaria now and when they reached it, Damaron saw a log building on a bench above the river. With his eyes fastened on it, he spoke to Lawson, "Maybe you want to stay here while I ride over and see if he's still there."

Lawson was uneasy. He scowled and said, "Damn it, Blain, I'm the sheriff in this valley, and I—"

"He'll have his chance, Mace."

"Just the same, I ain't sure I like it."

Damaron cut him a sharp glance. "We can argue it later. Right now I'm a hurry."

He left the sheriff there with his mouth half open, and rode on. Wariness was in him now and as he approached the log building he saw Lacey's horse tied to the rack and knew the man was still here.

When he reached the edge of the yard, Damaron pulled up and dismounted without once taking his eyes from the doorway of the store. He left his horse with reins trailing and started across the yard, walking slowly. His holster was not in the right position and he adjusted it without looking down.

"Lacey," he called into the stillness. "Come out."

There was no answer, but presently he heard the sound a chair might make as it was shoved back. A moment later a man appeared in the doorway and sunlight fell across his hard face. Indecision held him briefly, then he hitched up his gunbelt and stepped into the yard, moving toward Damaron.

"I'm tired of running, Damaron."

"I'm tired of chasing you, Lacey."

The man began to move faster as if now that he knew there was no way out he was in a hurry to get it over with. "Wasn't for you," he said, "I could have got away with it."

"You do all right at back-shooting," Damaron said tone-

8

lessly. "Let's see how good you are when you're looking a man in the face."

A muscle jerked in Lacey's face and Damaron watched him, waiting until the man's hand had closed over the bone grips of his pistol. Then Damaron drew his own gun, pulled it with the same incredible speed that had beaten better men than he was facing now.

Lacey sent one shot into the dust, but his eyes were already glazing when he squeezed the trigger. Damaron's bullet slammed him back against the front of the store and he remained there for a brief interval, his gun dangling in his hand. Then his fingers opened and the gun fell to the ground and a moment later Al Lacey followed it, his eyes fixed on the last thing he would ever see—the bullet hole in his shirt pocket.

The last echoes of the shots died and silence came back while Damaron blew smoke from the muzzle of his gun and put it back in his holster. He looked at Lacey and he felt nothing. A sound behind him caused him to turn and he saw Mace Lawson riding across the yard.

The sheriff climbed down, and moving past Damaron, went to the front of the store where he knelt beside Lacey and made a brief examination.

A woman appeared in the doorway of the store and Damaron looked at her and she looked at him. She was not what you'd expect to find stuck out here in the middle of nowhere. She was tall and full-breasted and her hair was black, pulled back tightly from her smooth forehead. But it was her eyes that held Damaron, steady dark eyes that had just witnessed a killing and yet there was no fear in them.

Without looking away from Damaron, the woman spoke to Lawson. "I was watching from the window. It was Lacey who went for his gun first."

"Yeah," Lawson said, getting to his feet. "I was watching it, too." He shook his head, unbelieving. "I've known men who were supposed to be fast, but I never saw nothing like this."

"I could stand a fresh drink of water," Damaron said, still looking at the girl.

"Come inside," she said. "I'll get you one."

Lawson did not offer to introduce them. He glanced down at the body, shook his head again, and said, "I guess I better take him into town."

"I can do it," Damaron told him. "You were on your way somewhere."

"I can tend to that later," Lawson said. "We'll have to have an inquest, so you better come along. 'Course it'll just be routine."

Damaron stood looking at the doorway, fingering the stubble on his cheeks. "I'll be back in a minute," he said, and went into the store. There was a small counter at the back of the room; shelves lined the walls. Behind the counter was a door that evidently led to the living quarters. The woman was coming through it, a pitcher in one hand, a glass in the other. She set the pitcher on the counter and Damaron watched her fill the glass.

"My name's Damaron," he said. "Blain Damaron."

"I'm Mina Vail," she said, handing him the glass. "Lacey stopped here for food."

"He knew I was getting close," Damaron told her. "Maybe he decided it might as well be here as somewhere else."

There had been no criticism in her tone nor in her eyes, and that was something Damaron was not used to. His clothes were dusty and he needed a shave and a bath, but she did not seem aware of these things. Her gaze remained on his face, probing as if she were trying to see what lay beneath the surface.

"Do you plan to stop in Candelaria?"

Damaron drained the glass and set it back on the counter. "Not long. I'll rest up a couple of days and then push on."

"Maybe I'll see you in town," she said. "I'm coming in tonight for the dance."

"Thanks for the drink," Damaron said, and his eyes clung to her for a moment longer before he turned toward the door.

When they had loaded Lacey's body on his horse, Damaron and Lawson started for town. Damaron looked back once and saw Mina Vail standing in the doorway, a small breeze pressing her dress against her slender body.

"Some looker, ain't she?" Lawson said.

"She got a husband around somewhere?"

"Not anymore."

"What happened to him?"

"Came here with bad lungs, figured maybe the climate would help him, but I guess he waited too long. Died about a year ago and since then Mina's been running the store by herself."

"Most women," Damaron said musingly, "would be afraid to stay out here alone."

"Mentioned something like that to her once," Lawson

said. "Told me she had a gun around and that she knew how to use it."

They rode a short distance in silence, then the sheriff glanced at Lacey's body which they had tied face down across the saddle of his horse. He asked, "You figure to ship the body back to Texas?"

Damaron shook his head. "We'll bury him in Candelaria."

"How much you get for the job?"

"A thousand dollars."

"And what will you do with it—go on a drunk and throw it away in some honky-tonk?"

Damaron reached for his tobacco sack, and smiled with one side of his mouth. "You think I was just a wild kid with powder smoke in his eyes, who ran away from home and turned out bad like his dad said he would. Well, you've got me pegged wrong, Mace."

"Yeah," Lawson said dryly.

Damaron looked ahead of him, staring out across the rolling land. "I didn't get in this business to see how many notches I could get on my gun."

"Why then?"

"Because it pays better than punching cows or breaking broncs. And the money I make goes into a bank. It'll buy me a ranch someday, and it won't be any two-bit outfit, either."

"Ever stop to think you might not live long enough to get that spread?"

Damaron shrugged. "It's something I don't worry about."

Lawson studied him. "How old are you?"

"Twenty-seven."

"And none of those men you've killed are causing you to lose any sleep yet, huh?"

"Nope."

"They will. You just wait awhile—say till you're thirty, and then see how you feel about things."

"When I'm thirty I'm going to quit. I'll have enough saved by then to set me up."

The sheriff stared reflectively toward the mountains. "I knew a fella once that was fast with a gun, built up quite a rep. Killed ten men, I think it was, before he got a bellyful and decided to change his way of living. Met a girl and they got married and he stopped packing a gun—at least he tried to, but there was always some young buck coming along and wanting to take him on."

Lawson's gaze stayed on the mountains and he wagged his head sadly. "No, they wouldn't let him quit and it seemed like he couldn't go far enough that somebody wouldn't come along and recognize him. Even grew a beard and changed his name."

Damaron said moodily, "Everything is a gamble. Anyway, I've dealt myself a hand and I'm playing it out."

They rode awhile in silence and when they came to Halfway Creek, Damaron's gaze followed the stream. He thought of some of the holes where he used to fish and he remembered the house at the upper end of the creek. He said idly, "What happened to the outfit?"

"Taxes were due and when we didn't hear from you it was sold to a fellow named Colby."

"The Perrys still here, I suppose?" Damaron asked, thinking of Kate and her daughter Ruth who had owned the outfit next to theirs.

"You know Kate wouldn't leave this valley."

"How's Ruth doing?"

"Growed up to be a real beauty."

They crossed the creek and rode on toward Candelaria. When they passed the turn-off that led to what used to be the Long S, Damaron asked, "The Stobaughs still around?"

The sheriff nodded and his face was grave. "Ira's been flat on his back for almost a year. Doc says he can't last much longer. When he cashes in there's going to be big trouble in this valley."

"Why?"

"Because up till now Ira's been able to hold those boys of his in line. Dirk and Lang have made it plain, though, that when the old man dies things are going to be different. They want the whole valley and they figure to get it."

"For what reason?"

"Because Lang's got it in his head that folks look down on him because his mother came from a Denver parlor house. He's let it twist his thinking to where he's got to prove to himself and everybody that he can be somebody big in spite of what his mother was."

It was something that held little interest for Damaron. Not far ahead now was Candelaria. When he got there he would send a wire, telling the man who had hired him that the job was done. He'd wait for his money, rest up a few days, and ride on to another town where somebody was looking for a man with a fast gun.

Chapter 2

CANDELARIA HAD CHANGED LITTLE IN THE SEVEN years that Damaron had been away. It was a small town with frame and adobe buildings lining a wide street. There was no railroad but a narrow-gauge line had been built as far as Silver, and a stage made a daily run from Candelaria to the mining town in the mountains.

When they had taken the body to the undertaker's, Damaron stabled his horse and went to the hotel. It was Saturday and quite a few people were in town, ranchers and their families, riders for the surrounding outfits. By the time he got to the hotel, people were stopping to stare and he knew that word of his coming was spreading fast. The uneasy glances some of them cast in his direction irritated him in spite of the fact that he was used to it.

A small, thin man standing on the porch of the hotel turned when Damaron came up, and hurried inside. There was a small lobby and a desk beside the stairway. The man was behind the desk, using the sleeve of his shirt to wipe dust from the register and smiling broadly as he watched Damaron cross the lobby.

"Yes, sir," he said. "Welcome to the Candelaria House. Good rooms and the best meals in town."

While Damaron signed the register, the man went on talking, "My name's Reebe—Sam Reebe. I run the hotel and my wife runs the dining room, and when it comes to serving meals she don't take a back seat to nobody."

"I'll give her a try," Damaron said.

Reebe reached for a key on the board behind him, so nervous that he dropped the key on the floor. He picked it up quickly and smiled again as he handed it to Damaron. "Number seven on the front. Best room in the house."

"Just so it's clean," Damaron said, shouldering his warbag.

Reebe came out from behind the desk, reaching for the warbag. "Let me carry that for you, Mr. Damaron."

The irritation was in Damaron again and he wondered why there were so many men like this one who were ready to kiss your behind to get on the good side of you. He said shortly, "Thanks, I can manage and I'll find the room without any help."

13

"Well, if there's anything you want," Reebe said, following him to the foot of the stairs, "just let me know."

Damaron had a look at the room, got clean clothes from his warbag, and went out. The barbershop was two doors down. There was a man in the chair and two waiting on the wooden bench. They were all talking when Damaron came in, but the talk stopped as though someone had thrown a switch. Angelo, the fat Italian barber, had cut his hair as a boy and he had always been one to laugh and talk a lot. He didn't laugh now and he didn't say anything. With his razor held above the customer's face, the barber looked as if he were posing for a picture.

Damaron said, "Hello, Angelo. What's the chances of getting a bath?"

The barber found his voice and said, "The tub, she's a-clean and there's a-plenty hot water."

While he was bathing, soaking himself in the big wooden tub, he looked at his gunbelt that he had hung on the wall. He thought how seldom it was that he took it off, how much a part of his life it had become. It was his life, he thought then, for without it where would he be? And where would it get him in the end? For the first time a small voice inside him whispered its doubts.

Damaron silenced the voice and got out of the tub. He smiled thinly, telling himself that he had let some of the talk Mace Lawson handed out stick in his mind. That wasn't good. He knew where he was going and he had gone too far to turn back now.

When he went back into the shop it was empty except for Angelo. The little Italian was shaking his blue checkered apron. He finished and held the apron, waiting for Damaron to get in the chair.

"Same chair," Damaron said, smiling. "Remember you used to have to tie me in before you could shear me."

Angelo smiled, but he was plainly not at ease.

Damaron looked at the shelf below the big mirror, his gaze running over the shaving mugs that lined it. Some of the names he remembered, some he didn't. And he recalled that Jim Damaron used to have a mug there with his name on it.

He climbed into the chair and lay back, waiting for the towel, making idle conversation. "How's the missus, Angelo?"

"She'sa get pretty fat."

"That oldest boy of yours must be about grown."

"Tony, he'sa go to school down in Denver. Learn to be a barber like his papa. He's a fina boy."

14

"How many kids you got now?"

Angelo counted them off on his fingers, naming them. Eight boys and two girls.

"My God!" Damaron said. "When you calling it quits?"

"Pretty soon now, we think, but my wife she'sa want one more girl. In the old country everybody hasa big families. Everybody laughs and sings and there is much happiness."

With the towel on his face, Damaron lay there, feeling its heat, letting his thoughts run. He guessed that most men were like Angelo, satisfied to make a living and raise a family and let it go at that. Happiness, he thought, was what everybody was looking for and he wanted it too. But it could wait a while, and when a man didn't have to worry about where his next meal was coming from he could be a hell of a lot happier.

When he left the barbershop, Damaron went to the telegraph office and sent his wire. Then he walked back to the saloon and ordered a beer, aware of the way talk in the barroom had subsided since he came in. The bartender served him and stayed to use a wet towel on the mahogany, watching Damaron when he tasted the beer.

"Cold enough for you?"

"Fine."

The man in the white apron was short and stocky. His face had an unfinished look and all that was left of his hair was two patches above his big ears. "My name's Morton Baird," he said, still wiping the bar. "Everybody calls me Mort."

Damaron took another sip of beer and in the back bar mirror he could see that a lot of the patrons were watching him.

"Own this place," Baird was saying. "Bought if after you left here."

"How do you know when I left?"

"Ever since you hit town, mister, nobody's talked of anything else."

Damaron felt the sourness stirring in him. He dug in his pocket for some change, started to lay it on the bar.

"Forget it," Baird said. "This one's on the house."

Damaron put the money back in his pocket and took another drink.

"Anything you want while you're here," Baird said, putting his elbows on the bar and leaning forward, "just let me know."

"Thanks," Damaron said, and glanced along the bar, wishing the saloonman would go and let him enjoy the drink.

Several customers at the bar had empty glasses in front of them, but Baird paid no attention to them. He got his unfinished face a little closer to Damaron's, and said in a low tone, "I don't keep any girls here, but if you'd like to have a little party, I could fix it up for you."

Damaron's patience was gone. He set the mug down and put a sharp stare on the saloonman. "Mort," he said. "You run off at the mouth too much."

Baird drew back as though he had been hit in the face. He said shakily, "Just trying to be friendly."

"I came in here to get a beer," Damaron said. "Not a lot of idle talk."

The saloonman turned and went quickly down the bar. Damaron looked in the mirror again, and he was no longer thirsty. He laid a nickel on the bar and went out, feeling the curious stares on his back until he was through the batwings. On the porch he paused to make a cigarette and he was conscious of the talk starting again in the barroom.

Beyond the town he could see the San Juan Mountains, an uneven line against the sky, and the smell of the grass came in to him on the breeze. It was cattle country, he thought and it would never be anything else. A fleeting regret touched him when he thought of the old homeplace out there on Halfway Creek. If he had come back after the funeral and paid up the taxes he would have a place waiting for him when he decided to quit. But he had cut all ties when he left here seven years ago and he figured he would do better to settle somewhere else.

The sun was low in the west, poised above the dark bulk of the San Juans while it sprayed the mountain tops with orange and gold. Be dark in a little while, he thought, and turned up the street. On his way to supper, he passed the sheriff's office, a flat-roofed adobe building, and Mace Lawson was just stepping through the doorway.

Falling in beside Damaron, the lawman said, "Holding the inquest Monday morning, but you don't need to worry about it."

"I'm not worried," Damaron said.

Lawson said heavily, "You ought to be in my boots, and then you'd have plenty to stew about."

"Always thought you had it pretty easy here, Mace."

"Have had up till now, but with old Ira Stobaugh ready to kick off any day, I'm beginning to wonder if I wouldn't have been smart to go in the harness-making business. That's what

16

my dad used to be and he tried his best to get me to come in with him."

Damaron was watching the street and he saw four riders appear at the end of it. They rode at a trot, two abreast, and when they were closer, he heard Mace Lawson curse softly.

"There comes the trouble," Lawson said sourly.

The two men in the lead Damaron recognized as Lang and Dirk Stobaugh. Lang was the older of the two brothers, a tall, heavy-boned man with a straight nose and a hard mouth. He rode a blue roan and he sat erect in the saddle, giving the town a resentful stare.

"They don't look much different," Damaron said. "Lang must be about thirty."

Riding on a buckskin beside his brother, Dirk Stobaugh seemed amused at the uneasy glances being cast in their direction. Lean and slab-muscled, he was not so tall as Lang and while his eyes held a certain wildness there was missing the dark brooding expression that had always been in Lang's eyes. But whatever Lang decided on, Damaron thought, Dirk would go along with him.

Before the two brothers reached them, Damaron and the sheriff turned into the hotel dining room. Lawson was puffing from the walk and his round face was slick with perspiration.

"I'll have supper with you," he said. "Unless you was figuring on eating alone."

"I don't object to company," Damaron said, making a brief survey of the dining room. "There's a table over in the corner."

They sat down, Damaron with his back to the wall as was his habit. And Lawson, commenting on this, said, "You see, you can't relax long enough to get a bite to eat."

Damaron let him see a faint smile. "I can relax and be careful at the same time."

Lawson picked up the menu and scanned it without interest. "If a man's all tightened up inside when he eats, it's bad on his belly."

"There's nothing wrong with my belly," Damaron said. "At least nothing that a T-bone and some French fries won't take care of."

When they had given their orders and were waiting to be served, Lawson kept glancing at the street and there was worry in his eyes.

"With a couple of good deputies," Damaron said, "you ought to be able to handle any trouble from the Stobaughs."

"Hell, I've had to build a fire under the county commissioners to get them to okay hiring one deputy."

"Well, one good man might get the job done."

Lawson put his elbows on the table and leaned forward, his eyes on Damaron's face. "There ain't nobody around here that'll take the job, nobody that's good enough." He paused and in a lower tone said, "At least there wasn't until you showed up."

Damaron had found little interest in the conversation and his gaze had wandered, passing absently over the other tables in the dining room. Now he looked back at the sheriff, half in surprise, half in amusement. "You trying to josh me, Mace?"

The lawman shook his head slowly. "I'm dead serious, Blain."

Damaron, seeing that he was, said, "What the hell do you take me for?"

"I'm still trying to figure you out," Lawson said quietly. "I saw you kill a man today without batting an eye, but I guess he needed killing, and from the stories I've heard most of the men you've killed have been bad ones."

"And what does that prove?"

The sheriff settled back in his chair, but his sober gaze clung to Damaron. "It might mean that you haven't gone so far that you can't mend your ways before it's too late."

Anger touched Damaron then, and he said, "If I pinned on a tin badge would that change things? Would it make the men I killed any less dead than the way I'm doing it now?"

The harshness of his tone caused Lawson to squirm a little, but he said steadily, "It would put you on the side of justice."

"At fifty dollars a month?" Damaron said, his voice thick with derision.

Lawson glanced down at the table top. "I might get them to go as high as seventy-five."

Damaron laughed softly and without mirth. "I get five hundred to a thousand bucks for a job, and you talk about seventy-five a month."

"A man ought to think of something besides money."

"Not this man," Damaron answered with quiet stubbornness. "I know what I want and I'm not letting nobody stop me with a lot of high-sounding talk."

Lawson was silent for a moment, then he sighed and said

with a dim smile, "Well, you can't blame a fella for trying, Blain."

Their orders came and Damaron watched Lawson while he was eating, thinking that the sheriff was a man looking for someone to pull his chestnuts out of the fire when trouble came. For ten years Lawson had worn the badge in Candelaria, a man who was good at back-slapping and fence-straddling. But Damaron doubted that he had ever been called on to settle any real trouble. A man who had grown fat and soft, Damaron thought, and who'd never had much courage to start with.

In spite of his shortcomings, Lawson was likable enough, and Damaron, thinking of the situation the lawman was now in, felt a little sorry for him. Not sorry enough though that he was going to take any two-bit badge-toting job. A man had to look out for himself and it took money, a lot of it, to get you anywhere.

When they had finished with the meal and were crossing the room, Lawson paused and spoke to a man and a young girl who had just seated themselves at one of the tables.

"Howdy, Ed," the sheriff said. "Evening, Ruth." And with a glance at Damaron, he added, "Guess I don't need to tell you who this is?"

As a kid, Damaron had spent a lot of time around the Perry place, and he remembered Kate's daughter, Ruth, but he wouldn't have recognized her.

"Blain," Ruth said with a quick smile, and she came out of the chair, threw herself against him and put her arms around his neck. Before he knew what was going on she had kissed him on the mouth, her lips parted in a way that caused his breath to catch in his throat.

"Hey," he said, pulling her arms loose and grinning. "You're a big girl now."

She laughed lightly and there were little imps in her eyes. Green eyes that went well with her red hair. She was small and slender and she had filled out since he last saw her. The blue dress she was wearing was tight around her waist and tighter still across her breasts.

Just a scrawny kid with big eyes and a flat chest seven years ago, but her chest wasn't flat now.

The sheriff was saying, "This is Ed Colby, the fella I told you had bought your dad's place. Ed, meet Blain Damaron."

Colby was a slender man of thirty or a little under. He had a rather plain face and quiet eyes, but when he shook hands with Damaron, his grip was firm, and Damaron decided he was all right.

"Ed's taking me to the dance," Ruth said. "And if we can find something to do about Mom, we'll drive home alone and maybe do a little spooning along the way."

Lawson cleared his throat and Ed Colby, his face suddenly red, tried to smile.

"You see," Ruth said, looking at Damaron in mock seriousness. "I've turned out to be a little hussy."

"She's laying it on kinda thick," Colby said with a weak smile.

"I don't know about that," Lawson said. "Kate tells me this gal of hers is getting to be a problem."

"Speaking of your mother," Damaron said, "how is she?"

"Mom never changes," Ruth said, her eyes moving over Damaron's face with open interest. "She's down visiting with Mrs. Hines."

"I'll have to go down and say hello," Lawson said. "I tried to talk her into going to the dance with me, but you know how Kate is."

As though he thought he had to put in something, Ed Colby said, "If you get out Halfway Creek way, stop in, Damaron."

"Thanks," Damaron said. "But I won't be here more than a day or two."

Lawson started toward the door. "I'll see you folks around," he said, and left the dining room.

Colby looked at Damaron and nodded toward a chair. "I imagine Ruth's got a lot she would like to ask you."

"Seven years," Ruth said with mild reproof, "and not even a letter."

Colby was friendly enough, but Damaron knew he was spoiling something the man had probably looked forward to —taking Ruth to supper and then to the dance. "Maybe I'll see you later on tonight," Damaron said. "But right now I've got some business to take care of."

Ruth was giving him another warm smile. "Are you coming to the dance?"

"I might drop in for a while," Damaron said. He shook hands again with Colby, put his Stetson on, and left the dining room.

Chapter 3

OUTSIDE HE STOOD FOR A WHILE ON THE PORCH, noting that the street was dark now and that lamps had been lighted along its length.

With his back against the front of the hotel, he took his time putting a cigarette together, and he was thinking of Ruth and how much she had changed.

Remembering the way she had kissed him, he smiled wryly, and turned his attention to a large, two-story building a half-block down the street. A few rigs were already parked in front of the place and others were arriving. He heard a couple laughing as they passed in a buggy. Evidently unaware that they were being watched, the man held the reins with one hand and pulled the girl to him with the other. She made a brief struggle, giggling before she gave in and tipped her head back. Then a townsman, coming out of the darkness, started across in front of the buggy and the young man turned the girl loose and they both sat up very straight on the seat.

Staring after them, Damaron smiled, and wondered what it would be like to court a girl that way, the two of you taking drives and looking at the moon and making a lot of crazy plans. In his business you couldn't let yourself get too serious with a woman. Wouldn't be fair to her, drifting around the country, living in hotel rooms. Besides a woman could mess up your thinking, and he didn't want that, not now.

Man could always find himself a woman. Hell, there were plenty of them around that were willing to drink with you, have a few laughs, and let it go at that. They were the kind that didn't expect much from a man. They knew what he wanted and they gave it to him without feeling they owned him for the rest of his life.

Music was drifting down from the town hall now and Damaron listened to it, remembering that Mina Vail had said she would be in tonight for the dance. He took a drag on his cigarette and tipped his head a little to one side, liking the sound of the music. It was a waltz, a soft and stirring piece that got down inside him, reminding him how long it had been since he had really cut loose and enjoyed himself.

He flipped his cigarette into the street and turned up the walk. When he passed the saloon he started to turn in for a quick one, then changed his mind and decided to pass it up. Horses were lined at the rack in front of the saloon and he saw the blue roan and the buckskin that the Stobaugh brothers had ridden to town.

He remembered Lang and how he used to get off by himself as though he had a lot on his mind. Never was one to talk much and he always had a chip on his shoulder. They were going to school together when Damaron first heard the story about Mrs. Stobaugh, how old Ira had gone down to the Denver stockyards and wound up in a house on Holliday Street. He went on a big spree and when he sobered up he found out he was married to one of the girls. There were several versions of the story, Damaron remembered. Anyway Ira had brought the girl home with him and she had borne him two sons and made him a fine wife. But used to easy living, she hadn't lasted long after the second baby came.

After the way Mrs. Stobaugh turned out, folks stopped talking about it and Damaron was sure that nobody had ever looked down on her because of what she had been. She was a good wife and a good mother and that was all that counted. But one day in school, that big-mouthed Jones kid had thrown it in Lang's face.

"Everybody knows what your ma is."

Lang Stobaugh hadn't said a word, but Damaron would never forget the look that came over his face and the wildness that was in his eyes. He almost beat the Jones kid's brains out with a rock. Damaron shook his head, remembering. It had taken three of them to pull Lang off. He was like a wild man, and the Jones boy was never the same after that.

Damaron went on along the street, putting the Stobaughs from his mind as he neared the town hall. The upper floor of the building was brightly lighted and there were more rigs parked in front now, buggies and surries, a few wagons. He made his way through them, noting that a pallet had been spread in one of the wagon beds and a baby lay sleeping there, watched over by a boy of ten or twelve who sat with his back against the wagon side, playing a game of mumblety-peg.

Damaron climbed the stairs and when he reached the top a man was standing there, watching the couples on the floor. He glanced at Damaron and said, "Check your gun, mister."

"Sure," Damaron said, unbuckling his belt.

The man at the door reached for it, and then looked at Damaron closely for the first time. The looseness went out of the man and fear sprang into his eyes and he tried to cover it with a weak smile.

"Welcome to the dance, Mr. Damaron."

Damaron nodded and handed him the gunbelt, knowing the man was watching him as he moved to the side of the doorway. From here he surveyed the room, hearing the shuffle of feet as couples danced past. The orchestra was on a platform at the back of the room, five men who seemed to be enjoying what they were doing. There was a piano, a fiddle, a banjo, a bass fiddle and a guitar. The piano player had long hair and it kept getting in his eyes and he would throw his head back and never miss a note.

A gay crowd, Damaron thought. Having the time of their lives, and this was one night he was going to get in on it. He spied Mina Vail dancing with a sawed-off puncher who was holding her as if he was afraid she might break. They danced by and Mina looked at Damaron over her partner's shoulder. She wore a maroon-colored dress and he noticed the way lamplight touched her dark hair.

When the music stopped, he watched her walk to one of the benches along the wall and saw her glance again in his direction. The sawed-off man, his face very red and shining, was thanking her for the dance when Damaron stepped up.

"May I have the next one, Mrs. Vail?" Damaron asked, smiling.

"Why, of course."

The puncher looked unhappy. "Save me a waltz, will you, Mina."

"Sure, Willie," Mina said, but she was looking at Damaron.

Willie turned away with a scowl, then he spied someone across the room and his face brightened as he started in that direction.

"You see," Mina said. "He's forgotten me already."

"You didn't come with him, did you?"

She gave him a mildly critical stare. "I came alone, and if I'd wanted someone to bring me, don't you think I could have done better than Willie?"

"I'm sure of it," he said, smiling again.

The music started and they moved onto the floor. It was the first time Damaron had danced in a long time, but he had never been clumsy and with Mina Vail for a partner it was easy enough to keep in time to the music. With his face not far from hers, he caught the clean smell of her hair, and a sudden yearning stirred in him.

"You wouldn't need to come here alone," he said. "There must be a lot of men on this range who'd give their right arm for a chance to bring you to a shindig."

She smiled up at him. "You don't have to give me a build-up."

"I meant what I said."

She stopped smiling then, but her eyes remained on his face. "Maybe I spend most of my time alone because there are no men on this range that I care to be with."

"You sound hard to please."

"I know what I want, what I'm looking for, and in this valley I haven't found it."

Damaron had never met a woman such as this. He looked down at her and what he saw in her eyes warmed him, sent a ripple of excitement through him. He knew she was looking for something more than a night of fun and he wondered why she had been attracted to him.

"Me," he said. "I'm a man without roots—a man that makes his living with a gun."

"There is a difference between a gunman and a killer, and I knew when I first saw you today that you were no killer. As for you having no roots, that is not one of the things I'm looking for."

Damaron found his interest growing, but he didn't want her to get her hopes up, so he said, "There's jobs waiting for me. I'll be leaving here in a day or two."

"I'm sorry to hear that, Damaron. I was hoping to get to know you better. I think we might have a lot in common."

They went on dancing, silent for a time, and Damaron saw Ruth Perry and Ed Colby on the other side of the room. He lost them for a while, then someone else drew his attention. It was Dirk Stobaugh, who had just come in and was crossing the hall, followed by a lanky man with a hooked nose. Dirk was weaving slightly, and as he moved through the couples on the floor he shouldered some of them out of his way.

Following Damaron's gaze, Mina said, "That's Dirk Stobaugh and Rufe Ketchell, a Long S rider. Dirk has a habit of looking for trouble."

The two men had disappeared in the crowd and Damaron forgot them until someone started yelling, "Fight! Fight!"

The music stopped suddenly and people began leaving the floor, gathering in a corner of the hall.

"Come on," Mina said, taking hold of his arm. "Let's see who it is."

They joined the others and came to stop beside the lanky Rufe Ketchell who was talking encouragement to one of the fighters.

"Beat his head off, Dirk. Stomp him through the floor."

With Mina close to him, her hand still on his arm, Damaron looked at the two men in the center of the ring of dancers. One of them was Dirk Stobaugh and the other was Ed Colby, the man Damaron had met at the hotel dining room. From the expression on Colby's face, Damaron knew that he was finding no pleasure in the fight.

On the other hand, Dirk Stobaugh, his eyes bright with whisky shine, was going at it in a way that let you know this was to his liking. The two men came together and stood close, pumping blows into each other's stomach. Then Ed Colby, a slower moving man than Dirk, got through a right hand that landed on Stobaugh's chin. The blow straightened Dirk up, forced him to give ground.

Across the circle, Damaron saw Ruth Perry, her red hair like a flame in the lamplight. With her eyes fastened on Colby, she yelled, "Give it to him, Ed. Give it to him good!"

Damaron frowned, wondering if those flirty eyes of hers had caused this trouble. Then he went back to watching the two men as Dirk Stobaugh brought one up from the floor. Colby rolled his head and missed the full force of the blow, which might have ended the fight had it landed.

Dirk got ready for another wild swing, but this time Colby moved in on him with both fists swinging. Dirk was forced to retreat. He covered up and backed around the circle with Colby following him.

Damaron pulled Mina back a little as the two men came close and now Colby was concentrating on Dirk's face. The blows made a sickening sound that caused Damaron to wince. Some of the crowd moved back and he had a glimpse of a woman's white face as she turned away, unable to watch it any longer.

The two men were in front of Damaron now and there was only the thud of fists, the groans and grunts and the shuffle of boots. Rufe Ketchell, still standing next to Damaron, said, "Stop messing around, Dirk. Use your boots on him."

The fighters came close again and Damaron saw Ketchell put his boot out in front of Colby. Colby tripped over it, lost his balance and fell forward. As he was going down, Ketchell started toward him, saying, "I'll show you how it's done, Dirk."

Damaron reached out without thinking and caught Ketchell by the shoulder, whirled him around. He said quietly, "Let's don't gang up on him, friend."

A wicked temper was in the lanky man's eyes. "Mister," he said through stiff lips, "you're fooling with Long S."

That was supposed to be enough, Damaron thought, to let him know he was asking for trouble. He said, "I don't care who I'm fooling with."

Ketchell sized him up, and then with an oath and a sudden lunge he came forward. Damaron did not back up. He pushed Mina away from him and used his left fist on Ketchell first. That blow brought the man up short, and the second one, a right with all of Damaron's weight behind it, landed on the jaw. Bone cracked and Ketchell went down as if he had been struck by a club.

Mina moved back beside Damaron. She laid her hand on his arm and there was concern in her eyes.

Damaron rubbed the knuckles of his hand and looked back at the two men in the circle. Given a brief advantage when Colby was tripped by Ketchell, Dirk Stobaugh was wading in with renewed confidence. But the slow-moving Ed Colby was the better man, Damaron thought, and he was proving it tonight. Maybe Dirk had been slowed by too much whisky, but whatever the reason he was getting the worst of it.

Dirk went down, pulled himself up, and Colby dropped him again. This time Dirk was longer getting to his feet. He stood there, weaving slightly, wide open for the next blow that Colby threw. And that one did it. Stobaugh staggered back, causing the crowd to make a hasty retreat. His feet went from under him and he landed on his back and lay there, not moving.

Colby stood on wide spread legs, breathing heavily. He gave Ruth a tired smile and then the two of them came over to Damaron and Mina.

"Thanks for giving me a hand," Colby said. "But you better watch that Ketchell. He's a bad one."

Damaron nodded.

"Dirk tried to get me to come to the dance with him," Ruth said. "But I told him Ed had already asked me."

Colby said soberly, "He was sore about it and when he's had a few drinks he don't need much of an excuse to start a fight."

Damaron looked at Ruth Perry, wondering if she had been playing the two men against each other.

The music had started again and the crowd was breaking up, but no one had started dancing yet.

Colby touched a cut on his left cheek, and Mina Vail,

seeing it, said with quiet concern, "You'd better have that tended to."

Ruth examined the cut. "It's deeper than you think, Ed. Let's go over and have Doc Talbot look at it."

They started to turn away and then Colby paused and looked back at Damaron. "Thanks again."

Damaron stood there, Mina beside him, and watched Colby and Ruth cross the hall. Couples were moving onto the floor again now and noticing them, Damaron smiled and said, "No sense letting this spoil our fun."

At eleven o'clock, he saw her to her buggy and stood beside it for a time, neither of them speaking. He had half a mind to drive her home and he knew without asking that she would let him. She lived by herself and it was a long time until morning. He was tempted, but more than anything else he was tired, bone weary from a long, hard ride. Tonight he wanted that bed at the hotel and he didn't want anyone else in it.

Mina Vail sat there on the buggy seat, the reins held loosely in her hands as she looked at him.

"I ought to see you home," he said.

"I'm not afraid of the dark," she said with a faint smile. "I know you need rest."

He nodded. "Thanks for a pleasant evening."

"Would you like to come out for dinner tomorrow?"

He almost took her up on it before he caught himself, realizing he was letting this go too far. You've had your fun, he thought. Now forget it.

"Thanks," he said, "but I likely won't get far from the hotel tomorrow."

Disappointment showed in her eyes and then it was gone, and she said, "In case you change your mind, I'll be home all day."

They said good night, and he watched her drive away into the darkness. There goes a lot of woman, he thought, and then turned toward the hotel. Sam Reebe was not behind the desk, but Damaron's key was on the board and he took it and climbed the stairs to his room.

The bed looked good and he yawned as he removed his gunbelt and started to undress. Then he frowned, recalling the fight at the dance and his run-in with the Long S hand. A man who made his living with a gun shouldn't get into a fist fight where he ran the risk of hurting his hand. It could slow him down and it might cost him his life.

He unbuttoned his shirt, slipped out of it, and hung it on

27

a bed post. Then he held his hand up, the one he had hit Ketchell with, and examined it, flexing the fingers. The hand was all right, but supposing he had broken it? He had always been careful with that right hand, avoiding fist fights, but tonight he had been unable to stand by and see a man doubled up on. It bothered him now and he scowled, wondering if there was a softness in him that he wasn't aware of.

Sitting on the edge of the bed, he started to pull his boots off and then stopped as a knock came at the door.

"Who is it?" he asked, making no attempt to hide his annoyance.

"Lang Stobaugh."

Damaron swore under his breath as he got up and crossed the room. He opened the door and stood with one hand on the knob, looking at the man in the hall. There was no word of greeting from either of them, no move to shake hands.

"Want to talk to you," Stobaugh said.

Damaron went back to the bed, the springs squeaking as he sat down on the edge of it. He said dryly, "You and I never did hit it off, Lang, so what have we got to talk about?"

Lang Stobaugh walked to the center of the room, his bony face showing nothing as he looked at Damaron. He said, "I didn't come up here for old times' sake."

"Then what do you want?"

There was a chair beside the bed, but Stobaugh didn't sit down. He stood behind the chair, his hands on the back of it. "Maybe you've heard that the old man is laid up, going to cash in any time now."

"Yeah, I heard."

"When he dies, I'll be running Long S, and I've got some changes in mind. I'm bringing in more cattle and I'll need grass for them, a lot of grass."

Naked to the waist, Damaron sat there, liking this man now no more than he had seven years ago.

Stobaugh's eyes held a dark, brooding expression. "I'm going to own this valley, every damned acre of it."

"There's some folks around here that might not see it your way."

"Before I'm through they will."

Damaron reached for his shirt and got tobacco and papers out of the pocket. He said without looking at Stobaugh, "So, you're all primed and ready to make a move as soon as your dad's not around to hold you back. And you've come here to hire my gun?"

Stobaugh nodded. "I've heard you get a fancy price, but they say you're worth it."

Damaron shaped up his smoke with deliberate slowness. He said dryly, "The fact that we never had any liking for each other doesn't make any difference, huh?"

"This is a business proposition," Stobaugh said with a trace of irritation.

The dryness was in Damaron's voice again as he said, "Kind of free with your dad's money, aren't you, Lang?"

"Maybe, but money will get me what I'm after, and if it takes all he's got in the bank, I'll spend it."

Damaron got his cigarette going and looked at him through a cloud of smoke. He said, "I just finished a job and I'm not ready to go to work yet."

"I'm not going to haggle," Stobaugh said impatiently. "Name your price."

Resentment nudged Damaron. "Lang, you couldn't rake up enough to buy my gun."

"What do you mean?"

"I've got a strong stomach, but I don't like the smell of this deal."

Stobaugh's mouth slanted. "How can a gunslinger afford to be choosy?"

Damaron stood up, his patience gone. With level eyes pinned on Lang Stobaugh, he said softly, "This one can."

Stobaugh's face tightened and he stared at Damaron for a long moment before turning to the door. When he reached it he stopped and looked at Damaron over his shoulder.

"They say you're a real tough hombre, but after talking to you, I can't help wondering."

"Crowd me, Lang," Damaron said steadily, "and you'll get a chance to find out."

There was no fear in Lang Stobaugh, Damaron could tell. He doubted that the man had ever been afraid of anything or anybody. He stood there now, letting Damaron feel the weight of his eyes. Then he went out and his footsteps faded along the hall.

Damaron crossed to the washstand and poured himself a glass of water, thinking that it was the things that happened when you were a kid that made you turn out the way you did. Lang Stobaugh hadn't been bad to start with, but as soon as he was old enough to understand what his father had done, it had messed up Lang's thinking. It had made him mean and bitter and now he had to prove to himself that he could be somebody in spite of what his mother was.

29

The water was warm, but Damaron drank it and he remembered Stobaugh saying, "How can a gunslinger afford to be choosy?"

He never had trouble finding work and there were plenty of jobs in parts of the country where he didn't know anyone. Here it was different. He had been born and raised in this valley.

You'd better not fool around, he thought. Leave before you find yourself mixed up in something that you can't ride away from.

He went back to the bed and was again starting to remove his boots when someone rapped lightly on the door. Scowling, he got up and crossed the room and he was thinking, Can't a man ever get to bed around here?

He opened the door and Ruth Perry was standing there. She said, "I didn't think you'd be in bed yet."

Now what the hell does she want, he wondered. And then, conscious of his nakedness, he said, "Hold on a minute till I get my shirt."

"You don't need to bother," she said, smiling. "I like you the way you are."

He stared at her, curious, and wondered what was going on behind those flirty green eyes. When he turned to get his shirt, Ruth followed him into the room and closed the door.

"You'd better leave it open," Damaron said, watching her as he buttoned his shirt. "Some folks might get the wrong idea."

"About what?" she asked innocently.

"You coming to a man's room this time of night."

"Oh, for heaven's sake, Blain," she said, laughing lightly. "Everybody knows we're old friends."

Damaron smiled, and then, sobering, he said, "I don't know what to make of you. I sure don't."

"I told you I'd grown up to be a little hussy."

"I know what you told me, but I've got a hunch you're trying mighty hard to make folks believe you're grown up."

"It's fun to keep them guessing."

Was she so damned innocent that she didn't know she was asking for trouble when she rolled her eyes at a man? Damaron was quiet a moment, studying her. Then he asked, "Why'd you come up here?"

"Because I haven't had a chance to talk to you."

"I thought Ed Colby was taking you home from the dance?"

30

"Ed's still waiting to see the doctor. I told him he could pick me up here."

Damaron was still curious about her, but he said, "I hate to rush you off, but I'm so tired, I'm ready to drop."

"I just wanted you to know that there's nothing between Ed and me. We're good friends, and that's all."

"He strikes me as the kind that would make you a good husband."

"But I don't love him, and besides, I'm not ready to get married." She paused, smiled, and said, "Of course, if you'd ask me, I might change my mind."

"I won't be around here long enough to ask anybody much of anything."

She stood looking at him and then she glanced toward the door. "I guess I'd better go, before you throw me out."

He walked to the door with her and when he started to open it, she turned to face him. "Do you have to leave so soon?"

"I'm afraid I do."

"I wish you were going to stay a while."

He looked down at her, his face serious. "Forget me, and start thinking about Ed Colby."

"You think I'm just an empty-headed kid, don't you?"

"I'm not sure."

She was close to him and she said softly, "Give me a chance and I'll show you that I'm grown up."

"You don't want to keep Colby waiting," Damaron said. "Good night."

When she had gone, he lost no time undressing, but he was still thinking of her and wondering what she would have done if he had suggested she spend the night with him. Would she have jumped at the chance, or would she have run like a scared rabbit?

He got in bed and lay for a time staring into the darkness, thinking now of Lang Stobaugh and of the trouble that Stobaugh was going to bring to this valley.

Forget it, Damaron. It's not your fight.

He turned over and went to sleep.

31

Chapter 4

SAM REEBE, THE HOTEL MAN, WAS BEHIND HIS
desk reading a newspaper when Damaron came downstairs
the next morning.

"Morning, Mr. Damaron," Reebe said. "How was the bed?"

"Don't think I turned over once all night," Damaron told
him, glancing toward the dining room. "Right now I need
some coffee."

Reebe looked at the clock on the wall. "The missus will
be open about another hour. Then she'll close long enough
to go to church. Wouldn't miss the services for nothing, that
woman."

After a breakfast of ham and eggs, Damaron left the hotel
and started for the telegraph office. Few people were on the
street and Sunday quiet lay over the town. He passed the
furniture store which also served as undertaking parlor, and
he thought briefly of Al Lacey, lying in a plain pine box.

He walked on and when he came to the hardware store,
he stopped and looked in the window, remembering how the
gun had lain there among the other articles on display. A
Colt .45 with bone grips. He recalled the way he used to
come to town and stand in front of the window, admiring
the weapon, and how he had started saving his money to
buy it.

Jess Hines, who owned the store, had refused to sell it to
him at first. "You're too young to be fooling with guns,
Blain," he said. "Besides, your pa would have my hide if he
found out."

"I want that gun, Jess, and if you don't let me have it,
I'll give the money to somebody else and have them buy it
for me."

"Well, you can't say I didn't try to talk you out of it."

No one could have talked him out of it, Damaron thought.
He had taken the gun home and hidden it in the barn. But
every chance he got, he took it out and went down on the
creek to practice. It was there that his father had found him
one day and the licking was something he would never forget. It hadn't changed his mind about guns, though, only
made him more determined.

It wasn't just the gun that had come between him and his

32

father, he told himself as he turned away from the window. They never had seen things alike.

He came to the telegraph office and turned in, waiting at the counter for the operator who was busy at the clicking key. The man glanced up, and recognizing Damaron, dropped his pencil and came quickly.

"Any answer to my wire?" Damaron asked.

The operator shook his head. "Nothing yet, but I'll let you know as soon as word comes in."

"Thanks," Damaron said, and turned away, thinking that he should have heard from his man in Texas by now.

Returning to the hotel, he took a chair on the long front porch and settled back. From here he had a good view of the street and he sat there idly watching the arrival of wagons and buggies. Ranchers, some of whom looked uncomfortable in their Sunday clothes, drove their families toward the white frame building on the edge of town.

The bell atop the church was ringing, and hearing it, Damaron was reminded of the last time he had listened to a sermon. He was in Wyoming at the time, waiting to see a man who had sent for him to do a job. Hanging around the saloon he had gotten friendly with one of the girls, and when Sunday came, and because he had nothing else to do, he let her talk him into going to church with her.

He smiled wryly now, recalling how she had sat there, quiet as could be while the preacher talked, and before it was over she was crying and taking on something awful. It wasn't anything unusual, the bartender told Damaron later. Happened every Sunday, but that same night she was wearing her paint again and wiggling for the boys.

Thinking about it, Damaron chuckled, and then sobered as he caught sight of a woman coming down the street. He recognized her at once. It was Kate Perry, Ruth's mother. Buxom and large-boned, she wore a plain black dress and high buttoned shoes. By the time she reached the hotel there was a trace of perspiration on her smooth, ruddy face.

Damaron stood up, smiling, "Howdy, Kate."

"You long, lanky galoot," she said, stepping onto the porch. "Why haven't you been to see me?"

"I'd have got around to it," he said. "Have a seat."

She dropped into the chair next to his and bent down to rub her instep. "I'll take boots any time," she said. "These things will ruin your feet."

"I saw Ruth," Damaron said. "She's sure growed up."

Kate nodded and sat back in the chair. "I wish she'd find

33

a good man and get married, so I could stop fretting about her."

Damaron reached for his tobacco sack, asking, "How's the outfit?"

"Still keeping me busy."

Shaping up his smoke, Damaron smiled and said, "I thought you'd be married again by now, letting somebody else do the work while you take it easy for a change."

"There's no man around here that'd have an old crow like me."

"I wouldn't say that. Why, I'll bet there's plenty of them would marry you in a minute. Mace Lawson, for instance."

"I've got plenty to keep me busy now without having to take care of Mace."

With his cigarette going, Damaron glanced toward the sheriff's office and saw Mace Lawson standing in the doorway. The lawman's gaze was on the hotel, and noting this, Damaron had a feeling it was more than old times' sake that had brought Katy Perry to see him.

Kate was silent a moment. Then she said, "Mace is a pretty good man, but he's up against something now that's too big for him."

"That's what he was telling me," Damaron said, studying the tip of his cigarette. "I reckon the county commissioners will give him some help when he needs it."

"There's nobody around here that they could hire."

"The trouble you're looking for may never come."

"It'll come all right," Kate said in a low, troubled tone. "As soon as Ira Stobaugh dies, there'll be no holding Lang. I've watched him grow up, seen him turn meaner all the time." Kate paused and shook her head. "In a way I feel sorry for Lang, because he's sick, but it's not a sickness any sawbones can cure."

Mace Lawson, still standing in his office doorway, took his watch out and looked at it. Then he put the timepiece away and with a glance toward the church, left the office, angling across the street toward Damaron and Kate Perry.

"Mace offered you a job, Blain," Kate said, watching him closely. "Won't you think it over?"

He shook his head. "I've got other plans. I'll be leaving today or tomorrow."

She was silent for a moment, her eyes still on his face. "I've been worried about you ever since you left, Blain, wondering where you were, what you were doing. I've heard talk, stories that I didn't like."

34

"Stories are built up, changed and twisted a little more every time they're told. I'm a gunman, Kate, but to me it's a job, and I've never shot a man without giving him a chance."

"It's hardened you, Blain, made you grow up too fast. Maybe what you're doing isn't wrong. I don't know. But it seems to me if the country is going to grow and someday become a land where we can all live without fear, we need to leave the killings to peace officers and let courts of law decide who's guilty and who isn't."

Damaron said quietly, "That day will come sometime, Kate, but it isn't here yet."

She looked at him and there was no condemnation in her eyes. "Blain, Mace Lawson is offering you a chance to get right with yourself, to do something that will help a lot of people."

"Man hasn't got too many years, Kate, and if he spends most of them helping others, he's liable to wind up in his old age swamping out some saloon." Damaron was watching a buggy roll past the hotel, but he could feel Kate Perry's eyes on him.

"You don't sound like the boy I used to know, Blain, the kid that was always hanging around my kitchen, waiting for me to turn my back so he could get his hand in the cookie jar."

Remembrance brought a faint smile to Damaron's mouth. Then he sobered and in a quiet, even tone, said, "A man has to play his hand the way he sees it, Kate."

With a heavy sigh, she said, "I suppose he does."

A townsman had stopped Mace Lawson and the two of them were engaged in conversation in front of the barbershop. While they talked, the sheriff kept glancing toward the hotel, and now he started once more in that direction.

"Morning, Mace," Damaron said when he reached the porch.

Lawson nodded and spoke to Kate, "We'd better get started or we're going to be late for church."

"Why don't you come along, Blain?" Kate said, getting to her feet.

Damaron rose and smiled at her. "Guess I'd better not. Wouldn't want to keep folks' minds off the sermon."

Lawson said soberly, "Kate drags me down there every Sunday, but I could get a lot more good out of it if those benches weren't so hard."

"I don't think an hour a day once a week is going to hurt you any," Kate said, giving him a sharp glance.

"I reckon not," Lawson said. "Anyway, the music's good, and I like to listen to Myrtle Harrison play the organ and sing. What's that piece I like so much?"

" 'I've Got a Home in Glory Land.' "

"Yeah, that's the one." Lawson smiled and wagged his head. "Myrtle can sure sing it pretty."

Damaron held Kate's attention. She said, "I'll see you again before you pull out, won't I?"

"I want to rest up a little, so I likely won't get far out of town."

When she had turned up the street with Lawson, Damaron sat back in his chair. The church bell was still ringing, the only sound to break the Sunday morning quiet. Unrest was nagging Damaron. Presently he left the porch and turned toward the livery stable, deciding he might as well take a ride.

On his way to the livery, he saw Dirk Stobaugh dismounting at the rack in front of the saloon. Dirk's face was marked from the fight with Ed Colby. His lips were puffed and one eye was swollen and dark-circled. In the act of tying his horse, Dirk stopped and looked toward the church. As he stared in that direction his face tightened and his mouth turned hard.

Damaron could see Ed Colby standing in front of the church talking to Ruth Perry. Colby was smiling, giving no indication that he was aware of Dirk Stobaugh. After a moment, Ruth took his arm and they walked into the church.

For a moment longer Dirk remained beside the rack, his narrowed gaze fixed on the church. Then he turned, and tramping across the saloon porch, shoved roughly through the swinging doors.

Damaron's horse, rested now, wanted to go and as soon as they were out of the stable, Damaron let him run a short distance. With the town behind them, the gelding settled down to an easy pace along the main trail leading through the valley.

Damaron had no destination in mind. He told himself he would just look the country over, see some of the old landmarks, and go back to town. In the hills he drew up on a rise and from a distance viewed the Stobaughs' Long S. It was a small outfit, not as large as some in the valley, but Ira Stobaugh was a man satisfied with what he had.

Looking the outfit over while he shaped a smoke, Damaron

pondered briefly on what Lang would do when his father died. Then, because it was of no concern to him, he lifted the reins and rode on.

He passed some of the other ranches, the Perry place, and he thought of Ruth, smiling as he contemplated the change seven years had wrought. Then his thoughts turned to Mina Vail and he remembered that she had invited him to dinner. He found the woman attractive and wanted to know her better, but the old caution was in him and it warned him now to be careful because a woman, at this stage of the game, could mess him up.

As long as he had come as far as the Perry outfit, he might as well ride on up the creek and see if the old homeplace looked anything like he remembered it. Wild plums, growing along the creek bank, reminded him of the jam Kate Perry used to make. Man, there wasn't anything better than plum jam and hot biscuits.

There was one of his favorite swimming holes up ahead. He remembered one time he had been in swimming and had looked up to find Ruth Perry standing on the bank, watching him. She couldn't have been more than eleven, a scrawny kid full of curiosity. He smiled, remembering how he had tried to get her to go on so he could come out of the water. But she had sat there grinning at him and refusing to budge. He guessed he'd have been in the creek till dark if her mother hadn't come along looking for her.

He swung away from the stream now, rode through a grove of quaking aspen, and the house was before him. There was a new shake roof, but other than that it looked the same. Made of logs that Jim Damaron had sawed and put together. Strong and well-built.

There was no bunkhouse, only a barn, a few outbuildings and a pole corral. As he rode past the enclosure, a young man was coming out the gate. He closed it and stood there looking at Damaron, a stringy youngster of nineteen or twenty. Hair the color of a new rope and just as stiff curled on the back of his neck. His face was thin, but the jaw was firm and his blue eyes were clear and set not too close together.

"Howdy," he said.

Damaron nodded and, folding his hands over the horn, said, "I used to live here."

"You must be Blain Damaron," the young man said with quick interest. "Ed told me you gave him a hand last night. My name's Meegan—Rollie Meegan. I work for Ed."

37

Damaron's eyes moved over the yard. "Was out this way and thought I'd stop by for a minute."

"If you're not in a rush, I've got a pot of coffee on the stove."

"Thanks, but I'd better get back."

When he started to rein his horse around, Rollie Meegan said quickly, "If you're heading for town and don't mind, I'll ride along."

"All right."

Rollie started toward the house. "Be with you as soon as I set the coffee pot off the fire."

"I'll wait."

Rollie went on, walking swiftly across the yard.

Waiting for him, Damaron's gaze strayed about the yard, his eyes lingering for a moment on the corral. He remembered he had helped his father build it and all the time he was digging post holes his mind was on the gun he had hidden in the barn.

That was all that had meant anything. He had gotten where he could think of nothing else. At night he'd lie awake, staring into the darkness, and all the time the rebellion against his father was growing in him.

As Damaron sat loose in the saddle there, his face softened with remembrance. He recalled the little buckskin his father had broken for him, his first horse, and how proud he was of it. And there was the house with its big rock fireplace. Used to feel mighty good lying on that bearskin rug in front of the fire.

He swore softly then, wondering why he had come here in the first place, why he hadn't realized there would be too many things here to set him thinking, to stir a longing in him and make him wonder how it would have been if he hadn't let the place get away from him.

He was angry with himself now, thinking, you start getting soft, letting sentiment work on you and you're done for, finished before you ever reach thirty. You can't afford to let that happen, not after you've been so damn careful up till now.

The sight of Rollie Meegan coming out of the house brought Damaron's mind back to the present.

"I'm all set now," Rollie said, smiling.

They rode out of the yard together, taking the creek trail. When they had gone a short distance, Rollie said, "Ed's gone to church, but I stayed to finish up the chores. We're going to the Perrys' for dinner." Rollie smiled again. "Sure fine folks, the Perrys."

Damaron nodded, his eyes on a big boulder up ahead. It was there he used to come to practice with his gun and he wondered how many tin cans he had shot at all told. Some of them were still lying around the boulder, rusty and battered, grim reminders of the countless hours he had spent here.

Not much older than this Rollie Meegan, he mused. A kid with fuzz on his face, learning how to handle a gun. Learning, he thought somberly, how to kill.

"You been with Colby long?" Damaron asked idly.

"About a year. Ed's sure a fine fellow to work for."

"He and Ruth Perry seem to be hitting it off."

Rollie's face clouded. "They've gone together a long time, and I know Ed would marry her in a minute, but Ruth won't get serious. She don't seem to care about nothing except a good time."

"She been going with Dirk Stobaugh some?"

"Not lately, that I know of, but Dirk used to take her to some of the dances. Guess he thinks he's got his brand on her now and she's not supposed to look at another man."

"Maybe your friend Ed changed Dirk's mind last night."

"I wouldn't want to bet on it," Rollie said. "From what I've heard, Dirk Stobaugh is the kind that'll let something like that licking stick in his craw."

"I reckon Ed showed last night that he can take care of himself."

"With his fists, maybe, but if it comes to a gunfight, Ed will be up a creek."

"No good with a six-shooter?"

"Naw, neither one of us could hit the side of a barn, and with big trouble with the Stobaughs shaping up, I figure a man's going to need some gun savvy."

They rode on and when they passed the turn-off leading to the Vail store, Damaron thought of Mina, remembering she had invited him out for dinner. He was tempted to go there now, but he wanted to get back to town and see if word had come from his man in Texas.

Rollie Meegan eyed Damaron's gun with a touch of envy. "If I was half as good as I hear you are, I wouldn't have to worry."

"That's where you're wrong," Damaron said. "A man never gets to the place where he don't worry about something."

They were in sight of Candelaria now and Damaron looked at the cluster of buildings, thinking of all the other towns he had been in since he left here. Big cities like Denver and Dallas where a man could have himself a time. But there were none of them that he'd want to live in.

When they reached the outskirts, Damaron sensed that something was wrong. An air of expectancy lay over the town. Rollie Meegan, making idle talk, fell silent, as if he, too, were aware of it.

They rode on, their horses' hoofs loud in the tense silence, and still out of sight of Main Street. Then the harsh, flat sound of a gun broke the stillness. One shot. That was all. And while sound was still echoing among the buildings, they made the turn and drew up with Main Street stretching ahead of them.

Men stood motionless on the walks, Damaron saw at a glance. They were staring toward the saloon. There near the hitch rack a man lay on his face in the dust while a few feet away, Dirk Stobaugh stood with a gun in his hand, looking down.

Chapter 5

THE COLOR LEFT ROLLIE MEEGAN'S FACE AND with a hoarse cry, he spurred his mount into a run. Damaron followed at a slower pace, knowing without being told that the man lying in the dirt was Ed Colby.

At a rack next to the saloon, Damaron swung down, watching Rollie Meegan who had left his horse with trailing reins. The kid had run to Ed Colby and was on his knees now, his stricken gaze fastened on Colby's still face.

Dirk Stobaugh, his gun still in his hand, looked up and his hard eyes swept the street in defiance.

"You saw it," Dirk said in a loud voice. "He had his chance."

A man standing on the walk beside Damaron swore softly.

"What happened?" Damaron asked.

The townsman spoke in a low tone. "Dirk was in the saloon, drinking and saying that nobody marked him up and got away with it."

Damaron nodded, remembering the dark, brooding expression on Dirk Stobaugh's face earlier today.

The townsman was still talking. "Dirk sent word for Ed to get a gun and meet him, so I reckon there wasn't nothing else Ed could do. Nice fellow, Ed Colby. Never bothered nobody, and now he's dead."

Dirk Stobaugh had holstered his gun now, but he was still standing in the same spot.

For a moment longer, Rollie Meegan remained on his knees beside Colby's body as if he were hoping his friend would open his eyes and say something. Then, as though the realization had finally hit him that Colby was dead, Rollie lifted his head slowly.

"Damn you, Dirk," he said in a low bitter tone. "Damn you to hell!"

Stobaugh stiffened.

Damaron stepped away from his horse and moved toward Rollie Meegan. He came up behind the kid, walking slowly, watching Stobaugh. If Dirk saw him, he gave no indication.

With his hot eyes fixed on young Meegan, Dirk said, "You'd better take it easy kid, before you wind up joining your boss."

Rollie Meegan wasn't wearing a gun. Damaron remembered his saying that he wasn't any good with a shooting-iron. But he wasn't afraid, and kneeling there now, his desperate gaze fastened on the pistol in Ed Colby's lifeless hand.

"If you're itching to square things," Dirk said tauntingly, "go ahead and pick it up."

Reach for it and you'll die, Damaron thought as he came to a halt behind young Meegan. With level eyes on Stobaugh, Damaron said quietly, "What's the matter, Dirk? Aren't you satisfied with one killing?"

Stobaugh's narrowed gaze swung to him. "You horning in again?"

"The kid's pretty worked up right now," Damaron answered. "He'd be a poor match for you."

Temper thickened Dirk's voice. "You poked your nose in last night where it didn't belong, and now you're doing it again."

"It's a bad habit to get into," Damaron admitted. "But I don't go for one-sided deals."

Dirk Stobaugh had enough whisky in him to make him mean, but he wasn't drunk, Damaron could tell. The man had tasted blood for the first time, and liking it, wanted more.

Dirk glanced at Rollie Meegan. Resentment was strong in his eyes.

"If you haven't had enough," Damaron said, "maybe you'd like to take me on?"

41

Dirk wet his lips and sweat made a bright smear on his forehead. He said sullenly, "One of these days you'll push your luck too far, mister."

"Maybe," Damaron said, his cool, steady gaze never leaving Stobaugh's face.

Boots pounded along the walk and a moment later Mace Lawson came up, his breath whistling through his nose as he stepped between the two men.

"All right, let's break this up."

With his eyes still on Damaron, Dirk said, "In case you didn't see it happen, Mace, there's plenty folks that did, and I reckon they'll all tell you it was a fair fight."

"Yeah, I saw it," the sheriff said sourly. "Tried to talk Ed out of meeting you, but he said it might as well be now as later."

Dirk sneered.

Lawson's fleshy face was slick with sweat. He said, "There'll be an inquest tomorrow."

"Don't worry," Dirk said. "I'm not going to run off." He gave Damaron an oblique glance and turned away, walking toward the saloon. Several townsmen standing on the walk moved quickly to get out of his path.

Rollie Meegan, still on his knees in the dirt, got up slowly. With grief-filled eyes following Stobaugh, Rollie said, "He won't get away with this."

The sheriff, worried and uneasy, said, "I know how you feel, son, but there's nothing I can do. Not a damned thing."

As if he hadn't heard, Rollie said in a low tone, "I'll get him one of these days. That's a promise."

Lawson said, "Get that fool notion out of your head and simmer down, kid."

A lot of people were in front of the saloon now, Ruth and Kate Perry among them. Ruth, her smooth cheeks pale, came over to Rollie and laid her hand on his arm. The kid took one last look at the body and let Ruth lead him away.

"This is a hell of a thing," Mace Lawson said, shaking his head. "And on Sunday, too, with folks just getting out of church."

Damaron reached for his tobacco sack. He said, "Did Colby have any kinfolks?"

Lawson shook his head.

"Then I reckon the ranch belongs to Meegan now."

"Yeah, it's his if he can hold it."

Last night in Damaron's hotel room, Lang Stobaugh had said, "I'm going to have this valley, every damn acre of it."

And remembering those words now, Damaron thought of Rollie Meegan and knew that alone the kid couldn't hold out long.

Four men carried the body toward the undertaking parlor in the rear of the furniture store. Lawson watched them a moment, then turned and put harried eyes on the saloon. He said, "Dirk killed his first man today, but I've got a hunch it won't be his last."

"You're the law, Mace."

"Yeah," the sheriff said with a ring of bitterness. "But what can I do about a deal like this?"

"You figure it out," Damaron said. "It's not my worry."

Lawson stared at him. "You talk pretty hard and from what I've heard you're as tough as they come. I saw you kill a man yesterday and it didn't seem to faze you none. But last night you gave Colby a hand at the dance and today you sided with a kid that didn't mean nothing to you."

"Don't get your hopes up about me taking that deputy job," Damaron said, letting him see a thin smile. "Just because I didn't want to see the kid get himself killed, don't mean I've had a change of heart."

"You don't like one-sided deals, Damaron, so what about the one that the Stobaughs are going to pull as soon as the old man dies? You think you can stand by and see a lot of innocent folks driven out of their homes?"

"I'm not in the habit of going around solving other folks' problems, Mace. Besides, I'll be long gone from this town by the time Lang Stobaugh cuts loose his wolf."

Leaving the sheriff standing there in the street, Damaron turned and went to the hotel. Sam Reebe, standing on the porch, said, "You sure made that Dirk Stobaugh tuck his tail."

Damaron went past the man without answering. He started upstairs and then looked back at Reebe, who had followed him into the lobby.

"Any word for me from the telegraph office?"

"No, not a thing, Mr. Damaron. You want me to go down and find out if there's anything?"

"Thanks, but the man said he'd bring it up."

"I don't mind checking. Wouldn't mind a bit."

The hotel man's eagerness irritated Damaron. He climbed the stairs and went into his room in a sour mood. He washed and dried, unable to get Rollie Meegan out of his mind. For some reason he didn't understand he had been drawn to young

Meegan, and that was unusual because he had never been close to any man.

Still using the towel on his hands, he walked to the window and looked out at the street. He decided the reason he had taken a liking to Rollie was because the kid was about the same age he was when he started out. Or maybe it was because Rollie Meegan was living in the same house Damaron had run away from.

A knock came at the door and when Damaron opened it, Rollie Meegan stood there, his eyes still dulled by grief.

"Come in," Damaron said. "Have a chair."

"I can't stay long," Rollie said. "The Perrys are waiting for me. I'm going out to their place for dinner."

"Can't anybody beat Kate Perry's cooking," Damaron said.

"That's what Ed always said. He told Ruth that if she was just half as good as her mother, he'd be satisfied." Rollie had walked to a chair, but he didn't sit down. He stood behind it with his hands on the back. "Just this morning, Ed was laughing and joshing with me, and now he's dead."

"Tough, but that's how things go."

"It just struck me," Rollie said, "that I walked off without thanking you. That's what I came up for."

"Forget it, kid."

"If you hadn't stepped in I'd have made a damn fool play and got myself killed like Ed."

"A man needs to keep a cool head when he's handling a six-shooter."

Rollie's eyes touched Damaron's gun, lingering a moment. Then he said, "I reckon you know all there is to know about shooting."

"I know some, but I didn't learn it overnight."

Rollie was quiet for a moment, his eyes on the floor. The rug, a red flowered design, was faded and in several spots the nap was gone.

"They don't come any finer than Ed Colby," Rollie said. "He gave me a home, treated me better than anybody else ever did." The kid stared unseeingly at one of the worn places in the rug, talking as if the words were only for his own ears. "I was just a drifter, riding the grub line, but that didn't make any difference to Ed."

Damaron sat on the side of the bed and took his time putting a cigarette together. "And now you figure on squaring things."

"I'm going to try. The sheriff's hands are tied, but Dirk the same as murdered Ed."

44

"You've got a ranch to think about, kid."

"Do you think I could go on, living on the same range with Dirk Stobaugh, knowing what he did to Ed, and not doing anything about it?"

"I guess you couldn't."

There was a tight, intense expression on Rollie Meegan's face. Then he caught himself and said, "Reckon I shouldn't be bothering you with all this talk."

He walked to the door and with his hand on the knob turned to look at Damaron. "Much obliged, mister."

When the door had closed behind Rollie Meegan, Damaron got up and put his cigarette out in an ash tray on the washstand. He walked to the window, watching Rollie go to his horse and ride out of town behind the Perry buckboard.

It was hot in the room and the sourness was working on Damaron. He wished again that the trail of Al Lacey had not brought him to this town. The knowledge was growing in him that if he stuck around much longer, his carefully laid plans would be shot to hell.

He went downstairs and had dinner, sitting alone at a corner table. While he ate he was aware of the uneasy glances, and he heard talk of the shooting. He remembered the strong words Rollie Meegan had hurled at Dirk Stobaugh there in front of the saloon, and he wondered if Dirk wouldn't remember them, too. Knowing the kid was out to get him, would Dirk be willing to wait or would he force Rollie into a fight now and have it over with?

The meal was good, but he wondered if the one Mina Vail had invited him to wouldn't have been better. And he would have had company, someone to talk to, someone who wasn't afraid of him and wasn't being nice because they wanted to get on the right side of him.

He remembered her at the dance, the dress she had worn, the way she had looked at him and the feel of her in his arms as they danced. A small excitement stirred in him and he thought, it wouldn't hurt to go out there for a little while.

He went to get his horse, and saw the telegraph operator come out of his office and start up the street. When the man saw Damaron, he started to run, and was out of breath by the time they met.

"Just came in," he said, handing Damaron the telegram. "Thought you'd like to have it right away."

Damaron thanked him and gave his attention to the yellow piece of paper, which read: "Out of town when your wire came. Am sending money order for a thousand dollars. Thanks for doing the job."

Damaron folded the telegram and put it in his shirt pocket, thinking that now there was no need for him to hang around Candelaria any longer. He could get his money when the bank opened in the morning and be on his way. Go somewhere and get a gun job that would pay him well, one he could do without giving it a lot of thought. Thinking wasn't good for a man and he had done too much of it since riding back to this valley.

He walked on and saw Lang Stobaugh dismounting at the rack in front of the saloon. By the time Damaron reached the saloon, Stobaugh was waiting for him on the walk in front of the place.

"Dirk told me what happened," Stobaugh said, eyeing Damaron narrowly.

Damaron said, "Figured you'd hear about it."

"I might have overlooked what you did last night, but when you took up that kid's fight this morning, you made it pretty plain which side of the fence you're on."

"You think so, huh?" Damaron said softly.

Stobaugh's face was hard. "I told you last night what I'm going to do, and I meant what I said."

"You're taking a long time to say something."

"All right, I'll make it short. If you're not going to work for me, I want you out of this valley, and I don't mean a week or a month from now."

Damaron's lips moved and made a thin, wicked smile. "I've got to hand it to you, Lang. You're not afraid to talk."

"And I don't talk to hear my head rattle."

"Then I reckon I can take what you said as a warning?"

Stobaugh nodded, his eyes steady, unblinking.

"Looks like I'll have to change my plans," Damaron said, and he wasn't smiling now. "I was figuring on pulling out in the morning, but you just changed my mind. I never did like to be pushed."

"You don't scare me, Blain, you or your gun or the rep you've built. There's plenty of gunslingers as fast as you and I'll bring them in, as many as I need. I've thought about what I'm going to do for too long to back down now. You better think it over before you make a big mistake."

"I've made my share of mistakes," Damaron said. "One more won't make a hell of a lot of difference."

He left Lang Stobaugh standing there and walked on, thinking that he had drawn a hand in the game whether he wanted it or not. But Lang had made it personal now, and a man couldn't walk away from a deal like that.

Chapter 6

MINA VAIL CAME TO THE DOORWAY WHEN DAmaron rode up in front of the store. She wore a pale green dress, long and full-skirted, and she was smiling.

"Hello, Damaron."

For a moment he just sat there, admiring her. Then he said, "You look like you're dressed up to go somewhere."

"No, I've been waiting for you."

Damaron liked her honesty. He said, "I told you last night I wouldn't be here."

"I know," she answered, still smiling. "But I was hoping you might change your mind."

Their eyes held for a moment before Damaron stepped down. When he had loosened his cinch, they went inside, walking through the store building toward the back. Entering the living quarters, Damaron stopped to stare appreciatively at his surroundings. The room was large and well-lighted by four windows. The furniture looked expensive and there was a bright patterned rug on the floor and lace curtains at the windows.

"I didn't expect anything like this," he said, holding his Stetson in his hand.

Mina took the hat and hung it on the tree beside the door, and said, "Howard picked out the furniture. He always wanted the best of everything."

"Howard was your husband?"

She nodded. "He was a gambler, and a good one, I suppose, because we were never without money. Before we came here, we lived in hotel rooms, going from town to town."

"That sounds familiar," Damaron said, grinning.

She looked at him closely. "You told me you'd been gone seven years, so most of your life was spent in this valley."

"Not the part that counts."

"Are you sure?"

"If I wasn't, don't you think I'd have come back before now?"

"Sometimes it takes a while to find out what you're looking for, what you really want."

47

Damaron said soberly, "I know what I want."

She looked away from him. "I thought I knew what I wanted, too, but I was wrong."

"How's that?"

She caught herself then, and smiled. "You don't want to hear the story of my life."

"Why not?"

"It would make dull listening."

They sat down on a horsehair sofa and he studied her, seeing the rich, creamy texture of her skin, and the dark sheen of her hair, pulled back tightly from her wide forehead in the Spanish fashion.

"I heard what happened in town today," she said in a troubled tone. "I didn't think Dirk would go that far."

"He's been straining at the leash for a long time," Damaron said. "He and Lang both. As long as old Ira was on his feet, he made them toe the mark, but I used to wonder how it would be after he was gone and the boys were on their own."

"Ira Stobaugh is a stern man. Perhaps he's been too strict with them, held them down too much." When Damaron didn't answer, Mina spoke again. "They say if you hadn't stopped it, Dirk might have killed Rollie Meegan."

"Meegan's just a kid," Damaron said. "But he has a lot of sand."

They were quiet. Then Mina asked, "Have you decided to stay now because of Rollie?"

Damaron shook his head. "I'm sticking around a few days, but it's because Lang told me to leave."

"Lang told you that?" she said, unbelieving.

"He offered me a job last night, laid his cards on the table. He wants this valley and he's going to hire gunmen to help him get it."

"But you turned him down, so he told you to get out?"

Damaron stared moodily at the wall. "If he had left me alone, I'd have been gone by tomorrow."

"Would you?" she said with a dim smile.

He frowned at her. "Do you think I was just looking for an excuse to stay?"

"I don't know."

"Well, I do," he said roughly. "I'll stay long enough to show him I'm not running from him. Just a few days, a week, maybe, and then I'll pull out."

The sun was gone now, but heat still lingered in the room, causing his shirt to cling to his back.

"It's warm inside," she said. "Would you like to take a walk?"

"Sounds like a good idea."

They went out the back way, following a path that led to the river. It was almost dark now and evening's silence, deep and peaceful, had closed in. Somewhere in the willow thickets a bird sent its lonesome cry into the shadows, and then it was quiet again.

Walking beside her along the river bank, Damaron was only vaguely aware of the water's low, rushing sound.

"I caught my first fish here," Mina said, looking out across the river. "Over there by that big rock."

Damaron smiled. "Pretty proud of yourself that day, I'll bet."

She nodded, her eyes still on the rock. "Can you imagine growing up without ever going fishing?"

"I used to go all the time over on Halfway Creek."

They kept walking slowly, and Mina said, "There was no place to fish near where I was raised."

"Where was that?"

"A town called Hays City, built in the middle of nowhere with sand and rocks as far as you could see." Mina's eyes were shadowed with memory. "I don't remember my father, and mother was a dance hall girl. I grew up in a saloon and when mother died, I stayed on, singing songs because it was the only thing I knew."

"That where you met your husband?"

"Yes, I was eighteen when Howard came along, just a drifting gambler, but young and handsome, and I fell in love with him, at least I thought it was love."

"But now you're not sure?"

"When you're young it doesn't take so much to please you. Anyway, I had never been out of Hays City, so it was fun at first, traveling around the country, seeing so many sights."

"Must have been kind of a letdown coming here."

"For Howard it was. He liked the big cities, but he never wanted to stay in one place for long. In a profession that usually has its ups and downs, Howard was lucky. He seldom lost and when we traveled it was in style."

On their left the river flowed swiftly, but Damaron was neither aware of the sound nor the smell of it. Mina held his attention and he looked at her, liking the firm line of her jaw, and her mouth, full and wide. She was his kind of woman, he told himself. She was used to knocking around. A woman without roots who would follow a man wherever he went and never nag him about settling down.

Mina was quiet for a time, her eyes on the path. Then she said, "Howard hated it here and all he could talk about was when he was well enough to leave. He always drank a lot, but that last year he was hardly ever sober. I suppose it was because he knew he was going to die."

"Now that you're alone, why do you stay on here?"

"I have to live somewhere."

"Must be three, four miles to your closest neighbor."

"The Saunders place is about three miles east of here."

"Too far for them to hear you if you hollered."

She glanced at him, smiling. "I'm not afraid of the men in this valley."

"Not even the Stobaughs?"

"Lang doesn't seem interested in women."

"How about Dirk?"

"Oh, I don't like the way he looks sometimes, but he's never bothered me, and I'm not afraid he will. Anyway, I have a gun in the store and I know how to use it."

They walked on a short distance, then turned back. When they reached the front of the store, Damaron heard hoof-beats and a moment later saw a rider coming toward them. It was a skinny, round-faced man wearing a battered hat and bib overalls.

"Hello, Mr. Saunders," Mina said when he pulled up in the yard.

Saunders nodded to Damaron and said, "I ran out of smoking tobacco."

"I'll get you some," Mina said, and turned into the store.

Saunders stepped down and stood near his horse's head, holding the reins loosely in one bony hand. He was plainly ill at ease as he looked at Damaron.

"Live over east of here," Saunders said. "Bought the old Hardesty place a couple of years ago."

Damaron rolled a smoke, his back against the front of the store. "I remember Hardesty," he said. "Didn't suppose he'd ever leave this part of the country."

"He didn't want to, but his missus got to ailing, and the doc said she'd be better off in a lower climate."

While he was busy with his smoke, Damaron looked at Saunders without interest. The world was full of this kind, he thought. Men who skimped and saved to buy a little piece of ground and then spent the rest of their lives trying to make it pay. They got married, raised a batch of kids, and kept hoping that next year would be a good one. But the odds were against them, against anybody who started on a shoestring.

But if a man had, say, ten thousand, he could start right, wouldn't have to make a loan at some bank and spend half his life paying it off. A stake, that was what Damaron was working for, and in just three more years he'd have it.

If you live that long, he thought, recalling words Mace Lawson had spoken.

Waiting for Mina to return, Saunders made idle talk and Damaron looked at him, thinking, the Stobaughs won't have much trouble with a man like this. He's no fighter. Hard working, maybe, but how long would he last if it came to gunplay? And that was what it was coming to, sooner or later.

Mina came out with the tobacco, took the money from Saunders, and said, "Mrs. Saunders get her pickles put up?"

"Finally did," Saunders said as he got back on his horse. "We'll have plenty of them things to eat next winter if we don't have nothing else."

Mina smiled, and Saunders, with an uneasy glance at Damaron, said goodnight and rode back the way he had come.

Staring after him, Damaron said, "You'll never get rich taking in nickels and dimes."

She jiggled the money in her hand. "It's a living."

Damaron was quiet for a moment, looking at her and aware of the excitement she stirred in him. You've seen her three times and already she's got a hold on you. That's not good and you know it.

After a thoughtful silence, Mina said, "I feel sorry for Rollie. He thought the world of Ed Colby."

Damaron nodded. "I think I'll ride over and see how the kid's making out."

She said without looking at him, "It'll be cooler later on."

"Maybe I'll drop back, but don't stay up, waiting."

She smiled. "I never go to bed early."

He got his horse and rode toward Halfway Creek, but he was still thinking of Mina, remembering the warm, woman smell of her, the shape of her mouth and the firm roundness of her breasts.

Damaron was not far from Halfway Creek when he heard the sound of shots, five of them, not far apart, coming from the direction of the Colby place. He reined up, listening a moment, and then put his horse into a run.

When he had crossed the stream he slowed down and

approached the house warily, half expecting to find Rollie Meegan lying in the dirt with Dirk Stobaugh's bullet in him. But the kid wasn't hurt, Damaron saw when he reached the edge of the yard. Rollie was standing in front of the house, looking at the smoking gun he was holding.

Damaron stopped his horse at the edge of the yard, darkness hiding him as he sat and watched Rollie eject the spent shells. The kid was standing in the bright moonlight and his face was tight. While he was reloading, Damaron rode across the yard, the sound of his horse causing Rollie to whirl around.

"Just me," Damaron said.

Rollie relaxed, and said, "I was trying to see what I could do."

"Not losing any time, huh?"

The kid shook his head.

Damaron swung down and walked over to him. "That Colby's gun you've got?"

"Yeah," Rollie said, glancing down at the weapon. "I reckon Ed used it to pound fence staples with more than anything else."

"Let's see it."

Rollie handed him the pistol and stood silent while Damaron examined it. A long-barreled Colt .45 with bone grips. Damaron balanced it in his hand, sighted along the barrel, and handed it back. "Let's see how fast you can get it out."

"Reckon I'm pretty slow."

"Everybody's slow at first."

"I'll bet you weren't," Rollie said, dropping the gun back in his holster.

"Sure I was," Damaron said. "Slow as Christmas." He walked to the house and sat on the steps, watching Rollie make his draw. The kid was slow and awkward.

"Settle down," Damaron said. "You're trying too hard."

Rollie listened to the instructions and tried to follow them, but it still took him a long time to get the gun out. Of course he might improve with practice, but Damaron had his doubts that the kid would ever be good.

"I can't seem to get the hang of it," Rollie said, coming over to the steps. "Funny, but I never thought there'd come a time when I'd need to know how to handle a gun."

"You'll have to be a hell of a lot better before you go looking for Dirk Stobaugh, that's for sure."

"I made a promise today, and I figure to keep it."

"What good is it going to do Ed Colby if you get yourself killed?"

When Rollie didn't answer, Damaron said, "I've heard it said that revenge is a bad thing."

"All I know is that the best friend I ever had is dead, and I can't satisfy myself believing like the preachers that Dirk'll get his on that day of reckoning."

Damaron looked at him, seeing the firm set of his jaw, and was again reminded of himself before he had left the valley. Seven years, but it seemed longer. A lot had happened since then.

"You've had a rough day," Damaron said. "I'd better go and let you get to bed."

"I couldn't sleep."

"Funeral in the morning?"

Rollie nodded.

"I'm going to be around a few days," Damaron said. "Since you're dead set on learning how to handle a gun, maybe I can give you some pointers."

"I'd be much obliged, and if you're staying, I'd be glad to have you bunk here."

Considering it, Damaron started to refuse. Then he changed his mind, thinking, why not? It would be better than that hot room in town and he wouldn't have to listen to that damned hotel man run off at the mouth. Then too, he would be closer to Mina Vail's store, and as long as he was staying awhile he might as well get to know her better.

"I've got coffee on the stove," Rollie said.

"Wouldn't mind having a cup," Damaron said.

They went inside; and odd feeling came over Damaron as he stopped and stood looking about him. The surroundings were familiar; only the furniture was different.

"Never used to like coffee," Rollie said, bringing two cups to the table and going back for the pot. "Ed drank a lot of it and he kind of got me in the habit."

Damaron walked slowly across the room, his face somber and his eyes still roaming. The fireplace was there, a little more smoke-blackened, but that was all. He had helped carry the rocks that his father had built it with.

They sat at the table which was covered with a red checkered oil cloth and sipped their coffee while a kerosene lamp threw shadows over the log walls. For a while they were silent and then Damaron caught himself, thinking, come out of the past and stop poking in the ashes.

He took another sip of coffee, and looked at Rollie. "Say you been with Colby about a year?"

The kid nodded.

"Where'd you come from?"

"Was born in Montana. Worked in a livery stable after the folks died. I didn't like it. Got where I just couldn't stand the stink and the flies, so one day I pulled out."

"Where'd you go?"

"First one place and another, just drifting mostly." Rollie tasted the coffee and set the cup back on the table. "Decided I wanted to be a cowhand, and I got kicked around a lot while I was learning. Started out as horse wrangler for a big outfit in New Mexico. Had a tough ramrod. Man, he was hard to get along with."

Damaron let him talk, figuring he needed to get his mind off what had happened today.

"I saw a lot of country," Rollie went on, "and then I wound up coming here. Ed didn't need a hand, couldn't afford one, but he let me stay, and it wasn't no time till he was calling me partner."

"Good graze and plenty of water here," Damaron said idly. "Was Colby lining up with the other ranchers against the Stobaughs?"

"Oh, there's been a lot of talk, and some folks are pretty worried, but nobody knows anything to do except sit and wait for Lang to make his move."

"From what I hear, that won't be long."

They drank the coffee and talked a while longer. Then Rollie got up and walked to the door and stood there looking out into the darkness. Finally he said, "I think I'll ride over and visit with the Perrys a little while."

"How's Ruth taking it?"

"Kinda hard. Reckon she's blaming herself some for what happened, but I don't figure she should. Dirk was just looking for somebody to tangle with."

"Yeah," Damaron said, but he wasn't sure about Ruth Perry. He drained the last of his coffee and got up, saying, "I'm out of tobacco."

"You can get a sack at the Vail store. Closer than going to town."

"Guess I'll do that," Damaron said, deciding that Rollie didn't suspect that it wasn't tobacco he had on his mind.

They rode a short distance together and then Damaron turned off, telling Rollie he would see him back at the ranch. Riding on toward the Vail store, Damaron thought about his decision to stay with the kid, and wondered if he was playing it smart. But it would only be for a few days—just long enough to let Lang know he wasn't tucking his tail.

Then he came in sight of the store and forgot everything except Mina. She was sitting under a tree in the yard and now she arose and smiled at him.

"You made it back."

He dismounted and walked toward the tree. When he reached her, he stopped and they stood looking at each other, neither speaking. Then Damaron reached for her and she didn't try to hold back. She came into his arms, came quickly as if her need were as great as his. And when he lowered his head her mouth was waiting.

Chapter 7

MONDAY MORNING, DIRK STOBAUGH WAS STANDING on the porch of the Long S ranchhouse when his brother Lang came out of the house.

"How is he this morning?" Dirk asked.

"About the same—a little weaker, maybe."

Dirk swore softly. "Damned if I don't think he's holding on just to spite us."

"Sure looks like it," Lang said, his moody gaze on the bunkhouse.

Dirk said sourly, "Doc Talbot knows he can't get well, but he keeps feeding him those pills."

"He won't last much longer," Lang said. "He can't."

Dirk put one shoulder against a porch post and let his hand rest on the butt of his gun. He said, "Have you talked to Bailey any more about buying his cattle?"

Lang nodded. "He wants to sell real bad and we can get those two thousand head dirt cheap, but Bailey won't wait forever for us to get the money."

"Two thousand head," Dirk said, smiling, "with what we've already got will make us the biggest outfit around here. Why don't you see if the old man won't let you have the money now before Bailey changes his mind?"

"Hell, I know what the old man would say. He'd tell me we don't need any more cows, that we haven't got grass for a bigger herd."

"We'll get the grass," Dirk said. "There's plenty of it here in this valley."

Lang said in a low, bitter tone, "All we can do is wait, and that's what I've been doing most of my life. I'm getting damned sick of it."

Dirk was quiet for a moment. The Mexican woman who kept house for them was moving around inside and he heard his father call to her. She'd go running, Dirk thought, the way everybody did when the old man spoke. Laying there helpless as a baby, but they were afraid to cross him, he and Lang both. Dirk wondered about that. Hell, there wasn't anything the old man could do now. He couldn't get up and use that strap on them like he used to.

Remembering those lickings, Dirk's face tightened and he thought, he won't never lay a hand on me again.

Rufe Ketchell came out of the cookshack, his jaw still swollen and discolored from Damaron's fist. Lang watched Ketchell a moment in thoughtful silence before he said, "It wouldn't take much to set Rufe off. Work on him."

"Hell, you're not scared of Damaron, are you?"

Lang shot him a narrow glance. "Don't start getting cocky just because you were good enough to down Colby. He wasn't a gunhand like Damaron."

"He's still only one man."

"I know, but he might cause us trouble."

They left the porch and walked toward the corral.

Dirk remembered the way he had felt in town yesterday, the way everybody had looked at him. They never had paid much attention to him, but it would be different from now on. He smiled, thinking, I sure made them sit up and take notice. That was what a gun could do. One day you were just old man Stobaugh's boy and then you showed them how you could stand on your own two feet.

They'd be pretty careful how they acted and what they said to him in the future, the whole damned bunch. Then Dirk sobered, recalling how Damaron had stepped in and made him back down. Just when he'd had the town afraid to move, that damned gunslick had to steal part of the show.

When they reached the corral, Rufe Ketchell was standing near the gate, rolling a smoke.

"How you feeling?" Lang asked.

"Better," Ketchell said. "But it still hurts when I open my mouth."

"He must have really hit you."

Ketchell flushed. "Nailed me when I wasn't looking."

Lang's stare was critical. "When you rode in here, Rufe, you said you were a tough hand. You gave me a lot of big

56

talk and that's why I hired you. Now I'm wondering if I made a mistake."

"I told you I used to ride with Boon Haxen, and I wasn't joshing."

"I know what you told me, but the first time you met up with trouble, you got laid out with one blow. That was night before last and all you've been able to do since then is get from the bunkhouse to the cookshack."

"I'm all right now," Ketchell said, shuffling his feet. "Hell, I was trying to help Dirk and how was I to know that gunslinger was going to jump me?"

Dirk moved closer and looked at Ketchell's jaw, and shook his head. "You sure it's not busted?"

"It's all right, I tell you," Ketchell said, flushing again. "Just a little sore, that's all."

Lang started to turn away. Then he swung back, facing Ketchell again. "I wrote your friend Haxen," he said. "I offered him a job, but he hasn't answered yet."

"Boon never turned down a job if the pay was right," Ketchell said. "You likely won't hear from him, but he'll come."

Dirk opened the corral gate, and said over his shoulder, "I'm going to see what's doing in town. You coming, Lang?"

"No, I want to be here when the doc comes, find out what he's got to say after he sees the old man. Take Rufe with you. He's not worth a damn sitting around here, nursing that jaw."

While they were cutting out their horses, Ketchell said, "It'll be good to see Boon and the boys again."

When Dirk didn't answer, Ketchell spoke again. "You think that Damaron's something. Wait'll Boon shows up."

They saddled and were ready to leave when Lang called to Dirk from the barn doorway. Waiting until his brother had ridden over to him, Lang said, "Don't start anything that you're not damned sure you can finish."

Dirk grinned at him.

"Another thing," Lang said. "Forget the women for a while."

Dirk frowned. "Why do I need to do that?"

"Because you haven't got any sense when it comes to something wearing a dress. You get worked up too damned much, and now's not the time for it."

Rufe Ketchell was grinning faintly as they rode out of the yard. Dirk, seeing the thin amusement on the lanky man's face, said sharply, "What's so funny?"

"Nothing, not a thing."

"Then get that grin off your face. Just looking at your puffed up jaw is bad enough, without you making it worse."

They rode on, silent for a time, and Dirk thought of Ruth Perry, remembering the time he had been hunting cottontails and had come upon her swimming in the creek. Didn't have a damned stitch on and he had stayed there in the brush, watching her for a long while. First time he'd ever seen a naked woman, and the picture stayed in his mind.

All white and soft looking, the sight of her had stirred a need in him that had grown and become a wild hunger. He had half a notion to stop by the Perry place now and see if she was home. He could have Ketchell wait for him, but then he realized it was too soon after the killing. Besides, Kate might come in and catch him and he didn't want to tangle with that old witch.

He remembered what his brother had told him then, and he scowled, wondering why Lang never cared about the women. Never had gone with any of them after he found out about their mother. Dirk didn't see why it made any difference what the old woman had been, but it was something that kept nagging Lang.

The thing that bothered Dirk most was that he had busted his tail ever since he was old enough to sit a saddle. Worked like hell and all he had to show for it was some of the scars from the old man's strap. They had made money and the old man had stuck it in the bank, doling out a few bucks to him and Lang once in a while, and giving them hell if they asked for more.

There must be a nice pile laying in that bank and as soon as the old man was gone it would belong to him and Lang. Lang could bring in more cattle and do whatever he damned pleased, but Dirk, first of all, was going to have himself a time with some of the girls around here.

They rode past the Saunders place and Ketchell, glancing at the house, said, "This is the first outfit you boys'll go after, huh?"

Dirk nodded. "But we won't stop here. We won't stop till we've got the whole valley."

"That'll make one hell of a ranch."

"We'll have to have a big crew," Dirk said. "And we'll need a ramrod. You play your cards right, Rufe, and you could land that job."

"Lang'll be running things, and he don't seem too sold on me."

"You could change his mind, Rufe—prove to him that

58

you're big enough and tough enough to handle any job that comes along."

Ketchell touched his jaw and stared reflectively across the valley.

"Of course," Dirk said, "we're not going to have anybody around that can't hold up his end of things."

"I ain't never had no complaints," Ketchell said. "You wait till old Boon gets here, and he'll tell you about me."

"It's going to take more than talk, Rufe."

"What do you mean?"

Dirk shifted his weight, trying to find a more comfortable position, and said, "You didn't see me messing around with Ed Colby, did you? I fixed him so he couldn't ever lay a hand on me again. That's what you've got to do—fix them good."

Ketchell felt his jaw again. "I was figuring on getting that Damaron as soon as I was feeling better."

"They say he's a whiz with a gun, Rufe. A man'd have to be pretty good to take him on and come out of it without any holes in his hide."

Ketchell considered it. He said, "I wouldn't mind having that ramrod's job you were talking about. How much you figure it'd pay?"

"A hundred, anyway, and that'd just be to start with."

"Sure sounds good."

Dirk didn't look at him. "All you've got to do is show Lang that he's wrong about you."

Ketchell thought it over some more, and then said, "If I took care of this Damaron, do you think that'd ace me in?"

"I'd be willing to bet on it, Rufe, and I'll tell you something else. It won't make any difference to Lang and me how you go about it."

"How about the sheriff?"

"Mace Lawson." Dirk laughed. "I had him so scared yesterday that he was shaking all over, didn't know what to do. Don't worry about Mace. He knows how it's going to be around here before long, and he's not about to fool with Long S."

"The saloon ought to be a good place," Ketchell said as if he were talking to himself. "I'll go there and wait and Damaron is bound to come in sooner or later."

Dirk nodded and smiled to himself.

When they reached Candelaria, Dirk was aware of the uneasy glances being cast in his direction. He and Ketchell rode slowly down the center of the street, past the sheriff's office where Mace Lawson stood in the doorway watching them.

Dirk grinned at the lawman and then looked away, letting his contemptuous gaze rove the length of the street. They pulled in at the saloon rack and while they were tying, Dirk saw several people standing on the porch of the furniture store. Ruth Perry was there and she held Dirk's attention for a long moment. As usual his eyes stripped the dress from her and he saw her the way she had been that day on the creek.

Standing beside him, Rufe Ketchell said in a low tone, "Now me, I'll take that Vail woman, any time. She's been married and knows what it's all about. I'll bet she could give a man a run for his money."

Dirk saw Mina now, standing at one end of the porch, talking to Damaron and Rollie Meegan. Looking her over, Dirk said, "She plays too damned hard to get to suit me."

"That's the kind that's best," Ketchell said.

"They're getting ready for the funeral," Dirk said. "Most everybody will go up to the cemetery, but it's not likely Damaron will."

Ketchell ducked under the rack, saying, "Come on. Let's get a drink."

Dirk shook his head. "I want to mosey around a little. I'll see you later."

Ketchell went into the saloon and Dirk drifted down the street, feeling the weight of his gun and enjoying the way folks were looking at him. He was Dirk Stobaugh now, a man to watch out for, instead of one of the old man's boys.

He came to the barbershop and through the window could see Angelo straightening some of the bottles on the shelf behind his chair. The shop was empty except for the little Italian barber, and after a moment's hesitation, Dirk turned in.

"Howdy, Angelo."

When the barber saw who it was he knocked over a bottle of bay rum and picked it up with hands that weren't steady.

Dirk grinned and then rubbed the back of his neck. "Reckon I could stand a trim."

"I'ma close up," Angelo said, "till after the funeral."

Dirk, seeing a chance to make something of this, said thinly, "I reckon you'd take time to cut my hair if I asked you."

"You come-a back later."

Dirk had half a mind to stick around and watch Angelo sweat, but he decided it might be a good idea not to go too far just yet. He gave Angelo a hard stare and went out, putting a swagger into his walk as he turned back toward the saloon.

There was a rig in front of the furniture store now and they were loading the coffin into it. Dirk watched them and it didn't bother him at all to think about Ed Colby. He'd heard folks say you felt sick after killing a man, but Dirk hadn't been sick. He'd felt a little fear, but that had passed and by now he had convinced himself he was pretty fast on the draw in spite of what they said about Colby being slow.

Damaron was still standing on the porch of the furniture store beside the Vail woman, and Dirk looked at Damaron, wondering how it would be if he was good enough to beat Damaron. Kill a man with a rep like that and by God, you'd really be somebody.

He frowned, not liking the idea of letting Ketchell take the credit for killing Damaron. That would make what he had done yesterday look like nothing. But he guessed he'd have to let it go because Lang wouldn't want him kicking up too much of a stink. Let Ketchell do it and Long S wouldn't have to take the blame.

Dirk turned onto the saloon porch and glanced over the slatted doors. Ketchell was the only customer and he stood at one end of the bar, nursing a drink. Morton Baird was busy sprinkling fresh sawdust on the floor.

With his back against the saloon front, Dirk rolled a smoke and watched them getting ready for the funeral. There'd be a lot of funerals around here, he mused, before he and Lang were through. Then he looked at Damaron and muttered softly, "Come on over, damn you. Rufe's waiting to put a bullet in your head."

Chapter 8

DAMARON, STANDING ON THE PORCH OF THE furniture store, watched them load the pine box in the rig. He stood apart from the others because he was not one of them and their troubles were not his.

He had ridden in alone, arriving as the coroner's inquest was finished. Rollie Meegan stood between Ruth and her mother and the three of them were starting toward the Perry buckboard. Mina Vail, standing beside Damaron, said, "I'll go with the Saunders."

He nodded and remained on the porch while the funeral procession got under way, lining out toward the hill back of town. Ed Colby, he thought, had friends here, but Al Lacey, the man Damaron had followed from Texas, had been buried with only the preacher to put him away.

The town looked deserted now and the only one Damaron could see was Dirk Stobaugh leaning against the front of the saloon. While Damaron watched, Dirk left the porch and walked without haste toward a café across the street. Remembering the thousand dollar money order he had waiting for him, Damaron went to the bank and cashed it and deposited the money.

Another thousand to go along with what he already had. Money that a fast gun had earned him, and he wondered now how many more times he'd have to use it before he was through. How many would he have to kill and was there one waiting somewhere who was faster than he was?

He put the thought from his mind and turned up the street, noticing again the empty, deserted look of the town. The funeral procession was still in sight, moving slowly up the hill and he stopped to watch for a moment before cutting across the street toward the saloon. He passed a store with a piece of cardboard tacked to the door—a crudely lettered sign that read: "Will be open after the funeral."

Damaron went on, and reaching the saloon, turned in. There was only one customer and that was Rufe Ketchell, the Long S hand. He was leaning against one end of the bar, absently turning an empty glass, and he went on doing it without even a glance at Damaron.

Crossing to the bar, Damaron watched the man, noticing Ketchell's swollen and discolored jaw. It occurred to him that Ketchell might try to settle for that, but it wasn't likely he would attempt anything here. Unless Damaron missed his guess, Ketchell was the kind that did his shooting in the dark or from the brush.

Morton Baird, the saloonman, was straightening chairs at the card tables, but when he saw Damaron he stopped and hurried behind the bar.

"Whisky," Damaron said, standing so that he could watch Ketchell.

Baird set a bottle and a glass on the bar. "It's what I drink myself," he said, smiling. "The best in the house."

Damaron made no comment.

"Guess nearly everybody went to the funeral," Baird said. "But I couldn't see any sense closing up. There's enough folks without me, and besides, Colby never spent any money in my place."

"That's the way to look at it," Damaron said. "If you don't get something out of it, don't put anything in."

Rufe Ketchell had poured himself another drink now and not once had he turned his head in Damaron's direction. Still, the man's presence bothered Damaron. Putting a sharp stare on Ketchell, Damaron said, "Is there anything sticking in your craw?"

Ketchell looked around, pretending to notice Damaron for the first time. The Long S hand shook his head. "I don't want any more trouble with you."

"I just wanted to make sure," Damaron said.

Ketchell turned back to his drink.

On Damaron's right the side door opened and a burly, red-faced man came in.

"I've got five kegs for you, Mr. Baird," the man said. "That right?"

"I ordered six," Baird said, starting out from behind the bar. "What's the matter with you people? Can't you ever get an order straight?"

Damaron glanced through the doorway at the beer wagon parked in the alley.

"Says five on here," the burly man said, scanning a piece of paper he was holding.

Baird crossed the room, frowning. "Go ahead and unload them, but I want to make sure they don't charge for one I'm not getting."

While the man unloaded the beer kegs, Baird stood in the doorway and watched him. The saloonman's back was to Damaron and Rufe Ketchell, and for a moment Damaron forgot the Long S hand. Now as his eyes whipped back to the far end of the bar, he saw that Ketchell had turned to face him and the man's gun was already in his hand.

Caught off guard, Damaron leaped back from the bar and whirled, drawing his gun at the same time. The roar of Rufe Ketchell's pistol filled the room and Damaron felt the bullet as it burned a fiery path across his left side. The heavy slug drove him back and he staggered along the bar, off balance and unable to bring his own gun into play.

Another bullet from Ketchell's gun dug a groove in the mahogany, and then Damaron, stopping at the end of the bar, dropped down behind it. Ketchell fired a third time, but Damaron was out of sight now and the bullet screamed past him.

Baird had ducked into the alley as soon as Ketchell cut loose, and now there were only the two of them in the barroom. Ketchell started along the bar, moving slowly, and the silence had come back now, heavy and full of danger. After a few steps, Ketchell drew up, a wildness in his eyes as he waited for Damaron to show himself.

Damaron crouched there at the end of the bar, feeling the blood soak through his shirt and cursing himself for not having watched Ketchell closer. You couldn't relax for a minute. He knew that, but he hadn't thought that the Long S hand had guts enough to try a deal like this.

With his gun in his hand, Damaron waited a moment, listening for the sound of Ketchell's boots, something that would tell him the man's location. He decided that Ketchell was waiting, knowing that he had wounded Damaron, but not sure that Damaron was too hard hit to put up a fight.

Holding his left hand against his side, Damaron called into the silence, "I'm still kicking, Rufe. You figured you could stop me with that one shot, but all it did was knock the wind out of me."

Ketchell began to back up, his mouth jerking and fear in his eyes. A spittoon was in his path and he tripped on it, cursing as he lost his balance. Then Damaron came up from the floor and at sight of him, Ketchell whirled and made a dive for the end of the bar. Damaron fired and the bullet, catching the Long S hand in the right shoulder, caused him to change his course. He went lunging forward, passed the end of the bar and slammed into a card table with such force that he lost his hold on his gun and it fell to the floor.

Damaron moved along the bar, still holding his left side while blood oozed between his fingers. He watched Ketchell, sprawled across the table, roll over on his back and he saw the panic in Ketchell's eyes.

"Don't kill me," the Long S hand cried hoarsely. "For God's sake, don't kill me."

Damaron's gun was up, his finger tight on the trigger, but he eased the hammer down and gave Ketchell a contemptuous stare.

"Not so tough now, are you?" Damaron said.

Ketchell didn't answer. He leaned against the table, groaning and holding his shoulder.

There was noise outside the saloon and a glance showed Damaron that a crowd had gathered on the porch. He recognized some of the men who had gone to the funeral. They must have hurried back fast, and now they were watching from a distance, afraid to come closer.

Someone said excitedly, "Here comes the sheriff."

The crowd fell back from the slatted doors and Mace Lawson, his black suit rumpled and dusty, came quickly into the saloon. He paused a moment, his troubled gaze taking in the scene, and then came forward. Morton Baird, who had evidently gone down the alley to the front, followed the sheriff inside, but the saloonman drew up and remained near the doorway.

"What happened?" Lawson said.

Damaron told him and Lawson listened with his eyes on Ketchell.

When Damaron finished, Lawson asked, "Did the Stobaughs put you up to this?"

"Damn it," Ketchell said. "Can't you see I'm bleeding to death? I've got to see the doc."

"You'll see the doc after I've got you locked up," Lawson said, glaring at him. "I want to know if this deal was your idea or somebody else's?"

Before Ketchell could answer, Dirk Stobaugh spoke from the doorway. "You trying to pin something on Lang and me, Mace?"

Damaron had put his gun away and was leaning against the bar. He looked at Dirk, standing just inside the slatted doors, and saw that Stobaugh's hand was close to his holster.

The sheriff went over and picked Ketchell's gun up off the floor. He said, "I'm trying to get the straight of this, that's all."

"Just because he works for us don't prove nothing," Dirk said with a sneer.

"It does to me," Damaron said flatly. "And as long as we're here looking at each other, Dirk, maybe you'd like to try finishing what Rufe started?"

Dirk's face turned dark and ugly and Damaron, watching him, knew that Stobaugh was tempted to try his luck. For a moment the silence was thick and heavy with tension, and then Dirk said in a low, cold tone, "Maybe someday I will try."

Damaron's voice, rough and taunting, asked, "How long do you figure it'll take you to rake up the guts, Dirk?"

Mace Lawson looked worried and uneasy. He said, "Come on, Rufe. Let's get going."

Ketchell staggered toward the door and the sheriff, starting to follow, paused and glanced at Damaron. "Better get down to the doc's office, Blain, and have him tend to you."

Damaron nodded without taking his eyes off Dirk Stobaugh. Dirk waited until Ketchell and the sheriff had gone out, then turned and walked slowly from the room and the crowd fell back to let him pass.

"Everything was all right," Morton Baird was saying to a townsman. "Then I went over to the side door and the next thing I knew it sounded like all hell had busted loose."

Walking to the other end of the bar, Damaron poured a drink from the bottle Baird had left there. The saloonman, hurrying back of the bar, said, "Let me get that for you."

Men were still on the porch and Damaron felt their eyes on him as he went out and turned toward the doctor's office. The wound still hurt and the entire side of his shirt was wet with blood. He saw Dirk Stobaugh get on his horse and ride out of town. Watching him, Damaron thought, I keep getting pulled in, deeper and deeper, and now I'm up to my neck.

Doc Talbot was a round-bellied little man who wore glasses that looked too large for him, and he had a habit of peering over the top of them. With his shirt sleeves rolled up, he examined Damaron, and said, "Looks a lot worse than it is."

"Yeah," Damaron said. "It could have been my hand and that would have fixed me real good."

The medico went to a cabinet, talking as he got gauze and swabs out. "This is the first time you ever been shot?"

"Caught a stray bullet in the calf of my leg one time. That's all."

"Lucky, I'd say."

"I guess I have been up till now."

Talbot came back and sat on the stool beside Damaron. While he worked, he said, "Ketchell's arm is in bad shape. I may have to take it off."

"He'd better be damned glad he's living."

The doctor applied antiseptic and Damaron winced from the sting. He thought, Lang Stobaugh wants me out of the way and he won't stop because Ketchell failed. He'll bring in more men; there's a lot of them around like you. The kind that'll do anything for a price. You've never been up against anybody like Lang Stobaugh before, so don't sell him short.

Talbot said, "I never did make any money off you Damarons, you or your father, either one."

"Were you with him when he died?"

"No, but I saw him that morning, stopped by on my way back from the Saunders place. We visited a little and Jim was feeling fine, laughed and said he'd live to be a hundred. Came as a shock to me when I learned later in the day that Kate Perry had gone over and found him down by the corral."

"Heart?"

The medico nodded. "Just played out on him. Happens every day. Folks you'd never suspect there's anything wrong with, going along and not knowing what a sick day is, and then suddenly they keel over like that." The doctor snapped his fingers, and, finished with the bandage now, he stood up.

"Fine man, Jim was," the doctor said.

Damaron didn't answer. His shirt was a mess, but he would have to wear it over to the store, so he stood up and put it on, thinking of his father as he buttoned it. He wondered what had made them different, why one wanted one thing and the other something else.

He paid the doctor and went out, stopping under the wooden awning to roll a smoke. Mina Vail, standing beside a rig a few doors down, turned when she saw him and came quickly along the walk.

"I just heard what happened," she said, stopping at the foot of the steps. Then she noticed his blood-stained shirt and her eyes widened.

"It doesn't amount to anything," he said. "How'd the funeral go?"

"Like all funerals." She looked at him closely. "Are you sure you're all right?"

"Yes." He glanced along the street. "What happened to Rollie and the Perrys?"

"Rollie drove them home on the back road." Then she said, "The Saunders are waiting for me. I'd better go."

He nodded and said, "Maybe I'll see you later."

She turned back toward the Saunders rig, and he watched her, remembering his visit to the store last night, recalling the warmth and softness of her and the feel of her mouth against his.

The cigarette was between his lips, unlighted and momentarily forgotten while the Saunders rig held his attention. He saw Mina get in; the Saunders children, a boy and two girls, crowded around her. Mina was smiling at them when Saunders shook the lines and the rig rattled down the street past Damaron. Mina, talking with the children, turned to look at Damaron and his gaze followed her until the rig was out of sight.

As he left the porch he was thinking, you could ride a long ways and not come across another woman like that. Then he glanced down at the blood on his shirt, wondering how long his luck would last. Not forever. He was sure of that. If Ketchell's bullet had been a little higher, a little more to the left, he wouldn't be standing here now.

Chapter 9

For the next few days, Damaron did not get far from the Meegan place. His side was no longer sore and except for an occasional itching he felt as fit as he had before Ketchell shot him.

Rollie Meegan spent most of his time practicing with a gun and it was usually the sound of his shooting that awakened Damaron in the morning. For a long time now he had been in the habit of sleeping as late as he pleased, but a man couldn't sleep with all that racket going on outside.

This morning he opened his eyes and lay there for a while, listening to the sound of the gun. He had almost forgotten that on a cattle ranch you got up before daylight and started the chores.

Sitting on the side of the bed, he rolled a smoke and let his eyes travel slowly around the room. He could remember his father calling, "Blain, get up." And he recalled the day he left, thinking he would never come back. Yet he was here now, sleeping in the bed that had belonged to a man who was dead, eating at the table with a kid that man had befriended.

He dressed and went to the stove, tucking his shirttail in on the way. As usual Rollie had made coffee and Damaron poured himself a cup from the smoke-blackened pot. Outside the gun was still going off. With the coffee cup in one hand and a cigarette in the other, Damaron went out.

Rollie Meegan was standing in the yard, shooting at a tin can he had placed on a stump. He nodded to Damaron and said, "Bet I woke you up."

"I had enough sleep."

The kid returned his attention to the gun and Damaron leaned against the front of the house, watching him while he smoked and drank his coffee. With grim patience Rollie was trying to learn and Damaron had shown him everything he knew; how to tie the holster down, to wear it on the thigh instead of the hip, how to fire without aiming. But after all there was only so much Damaron could teach him. Mostly it was up to Rollie.

Rollie put his gun in the holster, and turned to face the stump. For a moment he was motionless, his arm hanging at his side. Then he made his draw and Damaron grimaced at the way he fumbled the gun, taking far too long to get it out.

He hasn't got the knack, Damaron thought, and he never will have, not if he practices from now till he's fifty.

Damaron looked on, watching Rollie who was standing in a half crouch empty his gun at the tin can. None of the shots found their mark and the kid shook his head as he began ejecting the spent shells.

"You're still trying too hard," Damaron said. "You've got to loosen up."

Rollie said disgustedly, "It don't seem to make any difference how I go about it, I just don't get any better. I watch you and it looks easy, but when I try it I'm all thumbs."

Damaron finished the coffee and threw the dregs into the dust. He said, "I told you it wasn't something you could learn overnight."

Rollie began to reload, his face gloomy.

Damaron was thoughtful for a time. Then he said, "Maybe some men are cut out for one thing, some for another. I've watched you handle horses and I can tell you've got a way with them."

"Horse savvy won't help me settle for Ed."

Damaron reached for his tobacco sack. "I've got a hunch that if Colby could get in touch with you now, he'd try to talk you out of what you're figuring on doing."

Rollie finished loading and now his eyes held a trace of bitterness. He said without looking at Damaron, "All I know is that Ed's dead while Dirk Stobaugh rides around looking for somebody else to kill."

"Dirk will get his one of these days, him and Lang both. Their kind always does."

"Yeah, but they usually deal out a lot of misery before somebody stops them."

Damaron got his smoke going and asked, "Have you heard how Ira is?"

"Kate told me yesterday that the doc said he looked for him to go any day now, said that most men would have been dead a long time ago." Rollie put the last shell in and spun the cylinder before dropping the gun back in his holster. "Kate's pretty worried about it. She says Lang and Dirk won't wait long after Ira's gone."

"They won't bother Kate," Damaron said.

"That's what I told her," Rollie said, coming over to the house. "But you know how Kate is. She frets about everybody more than herself."

"Too damn big-hearted for her own good," Damaron murmured.

They were silent for a moment, then Damaron asked, "How you making out with Ruth?"

The kid got busy adjusting his holster. "I've been over there to visit a few times and you're trying to build it into something."

"You didn't go to see Kate."

"Maybe I didn't, but I can't make any headway with Ruth. Never been around girls much and I guess I act like a damned fool. Besides, all Ruth can talk about when I'm with her is you. She thinks you're something real special."

"Since I won't be here much longer, you don't have to worry about competition from me." Damaron smiled, and then looked at his empty cup. "I've got to have another shot of Arbuckle's."

Rollie fingered one of the empty loops in his shell belt. "I'm about out of bullets, so I reckon I'll ride over to Mina's place, and get a few boxes. You want to come along?"

"Sure," Damaron said. "As soon as I have another cup of coffee."

They had saddled up and were riding out when Rollie stopped and looked at the horse pasture, swearing softly. "That blue roan's gone again."

"That the one you was telling me about?"

"Yeah. The ornery cuss is all the time breaking out and wandering off somewhere."

They found the tracks leading south and followed them. Damaron, loose in his saddle, looked out across the rolling grassland, thinking that a man could hunt a long time and find no better place than this to ranch. He saw some cattle grazing up ahead and when they passed them, he said, "You've got water and grass here for a good-sized herd."

"Takes money to buy cattle," Rollie said, his eyes on the tracks they were following. "Ed used up what cash he had getting started, but he figured after another year or so he'd be able to buy some more stuff."

The trail led them to a rocky stretch of ground and then played out. While they were trying to pick it up again, Rollie said, "Rafter 7 is just over that rise. Maybe Miles Wendell has seen the horse."

Damaron nodded. "I could stand a drink of water, anyway."

They rode over the rise and came upon a log house, a barn, and corrals. There was a well in the yard and they drew up close to it, both dismounting. While Damaron was reaching for the dipper that hung on a rusty nail, he saw a man come out of the barn and walk toward them. He was close to sixty, gaunt and white-headed.

"Miles Wendell," Rollie said.

"I remember him," Damaron said. "He and my father landed here about the same time."

Wendell came up to them, nodding to Rollie, but the look he gave Damaron was cool and unfriendly.

"Hunting for that blue roan of mine," Rollie said. "You seen anything of him?"

Wendell shook his head. "I've been working in the barn most of the morning." He was talking to Rollie, but his sharp old eyes were on Damaron. Now he said, "So, you're still here?"

Damaron was holding the dipper to his mouth. He took it away and said, "Anything wrong with that?"

"Yeah, I'm not the only one around here that's wondering what's on your mind."

Damaron hung the dipper back on the nail and when he faced Wendell again he was smiling. "Seems to me that with the Stobaughs ready to move in on you boys, you'd have something besides me to stew about."

"Lang Stobaugh is going to be hiring guns, and you've got one for sale."

"Lang has already hit me up, but I turned him down."

"Maybe you're just holding out, waiting for him to sweeten the pot."

Rollie said defensively, "Just because a man's a gunfighter, don't mean he's no good."

"You haven't lived as long as I have, kid," Wendell said, his level gaze still pinned on Damaron. "I've seen a lot of gunslingers and I've yet to come across one that I'd be willing to turn my back on."

"You're entitled to your opinion," Damaron said mildly.

"You're damn right I am." Wendell's eyes were snapping. "I watched you grow up in this valley, remember what a time your old daddy had trying to hold you down. He finally gave up and said there wasn't anything he could do to straighten you out."

Rollie said resentfully, "You've got no call to talk like this, Mr. Wendell."

"Let him talk," Damaron said, still smiling faintly. "Let him get it off his chest."

Wendell stood there, stiff and straight in the sunlight, a battered black hat shading his leathery face. He said, "That's about all I've got to say, but nobody's convincing me that gunmen are not all alike. Maybe they don't start out the same, maybe some of them are choosy about the jobs they take, but that's just to begin with. Pretty soon killing is in their blood and they've got to keep doing it, the same as some men have to have likker every day."

Rollie said with disgust, "Come on, Blain, let's go."

Damaron walked to his horse and stepped up. Lifting the reins, he looked down at the old man and said dryly, "Thanks for the drink."

Miles Wendell stood there, scowling as he watched them ride out of the yard.

When they had gone a short distance, Rollie said, "You don't want to pay no attention to Miles."

"Always was a cantankerous cuss," Damaron said.

"Yeah, and with this trouble with the Stobaughs coming, he's suspicious of everybody and his brother."

They rode on, picking up the trail of the horse again, and Damaron tried to forget what Miles Wendell had said, but the old man's words stayed with him, bothering him more than he cared to admit.

A mile from the Wendell place, they caught sight of the blue roan, grazing on a grassy rise. Rollie had no trouble throwing a loop over his neck.

Leading the horse, they turned toward the Candelaria River and came a little later to Mina Vail's store. The Saunders children were coming out the door, one of them carrying a brown paper sack. Mina came to the doorway, calling after them, "You'd better go straight home like your mother told you."

"We will, Mina," one of them said, glancing back. "And thanks for the candy."

She was smiling as she turned to Damaron and Rollie, watching them dismount and walk toward the doorway. She wore a plain green dress with the sleeves rolled up and had a white apron tied about her waist. Damaron regarded her, noticing the color in her cheeks, and thinking that she would look good in any kind of get-up.

The three of them exchanged good mornings and went inside, where Damaron leaned against the counter, idly scanning the shelves while Mina waited on Rollie Meegan. She brought the boxes of cartridges and put them on the counter, asking, "Will that be all?"

Rollie nodded and paid her, counting out the correct amount. "I reckon I'd better be getting back," he said, glancing at Damaron.

"I'll be along in a little while," Damaron said.

Rollie went out and Mina's gaze followed him. She said in a low, troubled tone, "A week ago he was just a boy without a care in the world, laughing and having fun. Now look at him."

"He's growing up fast," Damaron said.

She looked down at the money Rollie had laid on the counter and Damaron saw the troubled lines in her face. She said, "All the ranchers are buying shells. I'm almost sold out."

When Damaron didn't answer, she said quietly, "I haven't seen much of you since that first night."

He reached for his tobacco sack and then, changing his mind, let his hand fall away from the shirt pocket. He said with a dim smile, "I'm afraid to see too much of you."

"The great Blain Damaron, afraid of a woman?" she asked with a hint of mockery.

"Don't let it get around," he said dryly. "Some folks might start wondering if I'm part human instead of all machine."

Her hair, black and shining, was, as usual, pulled back tightly from her forehead. He observed this and then, lowering his gaze became aware of the pulse beating in her throat.

Her eyes remained on his face for a long moment and she was motionless behind the counter. Then she said, "I just made a pitcher of lemonade. Would you like a glass?"

"Sounds good," he said. "This is lemonade weather."

He walked around the counter and they entered the living quarters. Mina took his hat and hung it on the tree beside the door. She started across the room, saying, "Sit down. I'll be back in a minute."

He crossed to the horsehair sofa and stood in front of it for a moment while he looked about the room. There were no pictures of her husband in sight, no guns or anything that might have belonged to him. When Mina came back, carrying a pitcher and glasses, he said, "I thought maybe you might have a picture of your husband around."

She set the pitcher on a stand and started filling the glasses, talking while she worked. "When Howard died, I disposed of everything of his."

"I was just curious to see what he looked like."

"Oh, he was handsome enough. Blond hair, blue eyes, and a little mustache that he was very proud of." She handed him one of the glasses, and taking the other for herself, sat down on the sofa. "He was very careful of his dress, wearing only the best clothes. He had a way of making people like him, a smile that would buy him anything."

73

"Sounds like you had a good man."

"Most people thought that, but we seldom stayed in one place long enough for anyone to find out what he was really like."

Damaron held the glass of lemonade and looked at her, seeing the small, rueful smile that touched her lips. Her eyes were on the wall across the room and now she said, "Oh, I don't mean to imply that Howard was bad, because he wasn't. In many ways he was like a boy that never grows up, spoiled, irresponsible."

Mina stopped talking as the drum of hoofs reached them.

"A customer, maybe," Damaron said.

She stood up, smiling. "Three customers already today. Business is getting better."

She crossed the room and Damaron, placing his half-filled lemonade glass on the stand, followed her into the store. A horse stopped out front and a moment later Lang Stobaugh came through the doorway. He started toward the counter, touching the brim of his hat to Mina, but not smiling. Then he saw Damaron leaning against the far end of the counter and he drew up and stood there, stiff and tense.

Damaron said tauntingly, "Why did you send Ketchell to get me, Lang? Why didn't you come yourself?"

Stobaugh's gaze was unflinching. "I've got plans, Damaron, big plans, and I'm not going to let you sucker me into a shoot-out at this stage of the game."

"A few days ago in town you made some strong talk, gave me a warning to get out. But I'm still around and I'm tired of waiting for you to make your move."

Temper was a hard shine in Stobaugh's eyes and for a moment Damaron thought the man would reach for his gun, here and now. That was what he wanted. Have it out with Lang instead of letting the man stay on the sidelines and send his hired killers to do the job.

At the other end of the counter, Mina Veil was motionless, her lips parted while she watched and the tension mounted and filled the room.

Then some of the stiffness went out of Stobaugh, and he said, in a tone low and full of menace, "You won't have much longer to wait, I can promise you that."

He turned away from Damaron then, and facing Mina, said "I came after some cigars. You know the kind."

Visibly relieved, Mina moved down the counter. She brought a box of cigars out and put them on the counter, letting Lang help himself.

"How's your father?" Mina asked.

"He had a bad night," Lang said with a glance at Damaron. "I don't think he'll last through the day."

"I'm sorry to hear that."

"A lot of folks are going to feel the same way," Lang said, and his brooding eyes touched Damaron again before he dropped some money on the counter and tramped out of the store.

Mina stared after him and when they heard his horse leaving the yard, she said, "I never knew a man so cold and unfeeling."

Damaron didn't answer. He listened to the murmur of hoofbeats fading and he remembered what Stobaugh had said that day in town: "You don't scare me, you or your gun or the rep you've built. There's plenty of gunslingers as fast as you and I'll bring them in, as many as I need."

He'd do it, too, Damaron thought, and knew he couldn't whip them all. He cursed the stubbornness or whatever it was that made him stay here. Somewhere there was a man who was faster with a gun than he was. There always was, and Damaron wondered if here in this valley he would meet him.

Chapter 10

MACE LAWSON LEFT THE HOTEL DINING ROOM and was starting back to his office when he saw the rider turn onto Main Street. It was unusual to see a man riding a horse that hard into town, especially in the middle of the day. Mace stopped on the plank walk and removed the toothpick from his mouth while he watched the rider curiously.

Now the man was closer, his horse's hoofs drumming loudly, and Mace saw that it was Andy North, the old-timer who had been with Long S as far back as Mace could remember.

Watching him pull up and swing down in a cloud of dust in front of Doc Talbot's office, Mace thought somberly, I reckon this is it.

Mace walked on, his dinner laying heavy in his stomach. He wished he hadn't eaten the dessert, but it was peach cobbler and he never could turn that down. By the time he reached the doc's office, he was out of breath and he stood under the wooden awning, puffing while he waited for Andy and the medico to come out.

He didn't have long to wait. Andy came first, a small, wiry oldster who was without a hat for the first time since Mace had known him. Evidently it had blown off during the wild ride from Long S, and Andy had not wanted to take the time to stop and get it. He went back to his tired horse now, his bald head gleaming in the sunlight, and stood there, watching Doc Talbot hurry toward the livery stable.

"I've got a hunch this is the day Lang and Dirk have been waiting for, Mace," Andy North said.

The worry that had been nagging Mace Lawson was with him now, strong and pressing. He said heavily, "I guess I'd better go out there."

"Maybe you could get a rig and pick up Kate," Andy said. "Ira was asking to see her when I left."

The sheriff walked on through the buzz of excitement that Andy's appearance had stirred. Jess Hines, standing on the porch of his hardware store, shook his head as Mace passed, and said, "Looks like this is the day we've all been dreading."

Mace went on without answering. He saw Doc Talbot drive out of the livery stable and turn right. The medico was leaning forward, using his whip on the team of matched bays.

When Mace reached the livery stable, Harry Stiles was standing in the doorway, staring along the street where the dust was settling slowly behind Doc Talbot's buggy. Stiles, a chinless, narrow-shouldered man, turned and looked at Lawson.

"You going out, Mace?"

Mace nodded. "I don't know what for, but he wants to see Kate, so I'll take a rig and stop by for her. You keep your eyes on the office while I'm gone."

"You haven't had anybody in jail since you sent that Ketchell to Canon City. Man, the judge didn't fool around with him, did he?"

"If Damaron had finished him off," Lawson said, "it would have saved the taxpayers the expense of keeping him locked up. And putting him in the pen won't teach him anything. I've seen too many like Ketchell, bad from the start, and they don't never change."

While they talked, Stiles got a team from the corral and Mace helped him harness them. When they had been hitched to a light rig, Mace climbed in. He said, "You've been working as part-time jailer for about a year, now, Harry."

"Little over a year."

"I've been giving it some thought," Mace said, settling himself on the seat. "Might be able to get you on as deputy."

"That's mighty nice of you, Mace," Harry Stiles said. "But I think I'll stick to shoveling manure."

"Hell, Harry, you don't want to do that all your life."

"Aw, the smell ain't so bad when a man gets used to it, and with trouble on the way, I figure I'll be a lot safer where I am than toting a badge."

"You're not afraid of a little trouble, are you, Harry?"

Stiles stood there, his hands in his hips pockets, and said, "A little trouble don't worry me, but I don't want any part of them Stobaugh boys."

Mace gave him a critical regard and drove out of the barn. Even old chinless Harry had turned the job down, Mace thought wryly. He had hit up everybody he could think of and as a last resort had asked Stiles, even though he knew that the hostler would make a poor deputy.

Traveling toward the Perry place, Mace tried to think of some way he could stop Lang Stobaugh from bringing violence to this valley. But he realized there was nothing he could do, nothing he could say that would change Lang's mind. The threat of going to jail didn't seem to bother Lang, or maybe it was because he knew the sheriff was a man incapable of enforcing the law.

Mace scowled, not liking to admit that the job was too big for him, but there comes a time when a man can't fool himself any longer. He had worn the badge for a long time, but he had never been called upon to handle any real trouble. Staring along the trail ahead of him, he thought sourly, a middle aged man grown fat and soft from easy living.

He came in sight of the Perry place and his thoughts turned to Kate. She'd had it hard all her life. Married to a no-account cuss who never did anything except hang around a saloon and play cards. It would have been a lot better for Kate, Mace figured, if that stray bullet had killed Joe Perry a lot sooner.

Left with a ranch to run and a daughter to raise, Kate had little time for anything except work. She could rope and ride and handle cattle as well as any man, and she could shoot, too, Mace thought, recalling the time he had gone to visit and found a grub-line rider high-tailing it away from the house with Kate's bullets kicking up dust around him.

Mace chuckled. That drifter had been trying to get a kiss from Ruth, or maybe it was the other way around. Anyway, Kate had walked in on them, taken one look, and gone for her gun. Mace chuckled again, wondering if that drifter was still running.

He sobered then as he pulled into the yard, remembering why he was here. He stopped the team and started to get down, but drove on to the barn when he saw Kate appear in the doorway. She wore men's clothes: linsey trousers, a faded blue shirt, and a shapeless black Stetson.

She had evidently been forking hay, for she held a pitchfork which she leaned against the barn when she saw the sheriff.

"Andy North came after the doc," Mace told her. "Andy said Ira would like to see you."

Kate started for the house, saying, "I'd better change my clothes."

"The way Andy talked, he hasn't got long," Mace said. "We'd best get on over there."

Kate nodded and climbed into the buggy, using a clean bandanna to wipe perspiration from her ruddy face. Mace glanced toward the house, and said, "Maybe Ruth would like to go along?"

"She went over to see Rollie Meegan and hasn't gotten back yet."

Mace spoke to the team and they drove out of the yard, taking the trail toward Long S. Kate was silent for a time, a sadness in her eyes. As she looked out across the valley, Mace studied her, thinking how much he had come to look forward to those visits with her, the Sundays when he went to church with her and they sat together.

Kate said, "I've been expecting him to go every day for a month now, and yet I've been hoping all along that he would pull through." She sighed heavily. "I guess he doesn't have much to live for, knowing he has two sons that don't care, that'll be glad when he's gone."

Mace said nothing and Kate was quiet for a moment. Then she spoke again. "What'll you do, Mace?"

"That's what I've been asking myself."

"Blain's still around."

"Yeah, but he's made it plain that he won't take a deputy's job, and when you come right down to it, you can't blame him. He hasn't got anything at stake here, and like he says, he can make a lot more money working for himself."

"I tried to talk him into it," Kate said. "But I can see now why he turned it down. If he had taken it he would have been proving to himself that he's been wrong about some things, and he doesn't want to admit that, not yet."

"I don't savvy him," Mace said, frowning.

"Maybe," Kate said quietly, "Blain Damaron doesn't savvy himself."

Mace spied a rough spot up ahead and pulled the team into the weeds at the edge of the trail to avoid it. When they were lined out again, he said, "Funny what makes some men the way they are. Take Lang Stobaugh, for instance. Maybe he would have turned out different if Ira hadn't married the woman he did."

"Mary Stobaugh was a good woman," Kate said. "I don't care what she was before she met Ira."

"Sure, I know that and everybody else around here does too, but you'll never convince Lang that folks don't look down on him because of it."

They rode on and when they reached Long S headquarters, Mace saw Doc Talbot's buggy in the yard. Andy North was standing in front of the house, his bald head covered once again by his dusty Stetson. He was looking anxiously toward the door while Lang and Dirk sat on the front porch, their faces showing no signs of emotion.

Mace helped Kate down, saying, "I'd just be in the way, so I'll wait here."

She nodded and crossed the yard, moving past Andy North, who nodded and touched the brim of his hat. Lang and Dirk remained seated, and Kate, with only a glance at the brothers, went to the door where she was met by the Mexican housekeeper.

Mace leaned against the rig and got his pipe out. While he was filling it, Andy North drifted over.

"Doc's still with him," Andy said worriedly.

Mace got his pipe going and glanced about the yard before giving the bald-headed little rider his attention.

"You've been with him a long time, haven't you Andy?"

North nodded slowly. "I don't know why I've stayed. Bet I started to pull out a dozen times, but I always ended up changing my mind."

"Reckon the outfit kind of got a hold on you."

North reached for his tobacco plug and held it in his hands for a moment, turning it over and over. He said, "Ira and me always hit it off. Oh, we got into some squabbles now and then, but we saw eye to eye on most things."

Mace's eyes were on the house. Lang had gotten up and was walking back and forth the length of the porch, pausing once in a while to glance inside, and then going on with his pacing. Dirk was still in the chair, his feet on the rail and his hat tipped forward so that the brim shaded his eyes.

Following the sheriff's gaze, Andy said bitterly, "Look at them, waiting like a couple of buzzards."

"You going to stay on, Andy?"

"And work for them two?" He snorted in disgust. "The first thing Lang will do is boot me off the place, so I'm going to tell him I'm quitting before he has the chance."

Mace was thoughtful for a moment, puffing his pipe and watching Lang. Then he said, "Maybe old Ira was too rough on them, Andy. Maybe that's the reason they're the way they are."

Andy was still holding the plug of tobacco. He started to bite off a chew, then changed his mind and dropped the plug in his shirt pocket. He said, "You don't know them boys like I do, Mace. I've been around them for quite a spell now, watching them grow up and seeing the meanness come out in them more all the time."

Mace's pipe had gone out and he reached for a match, striking it on the side of the rig. Without looking at Andy, he said musingly, "I remember when their maw was living and she used to bring them to town all dressed up in their little black suits." Mace paused and shook his head. "My God! Where's them years gone?"

"Sometimes I get to thinking back, and I wonder the same thing. Just don't seem like any time since I came up from Texas with Ira and we settled here and started building a ranch." A note of bitterness crept into Andy's voice. "And for what? So them two up there would someday have something that they don't deserve."

"Reckon a man never knows how his boys will turn out."

"Ira knew a long time ago because he told me so. He knew, but he kept hoping all along that he was wrong, that maybe they'd change and he'd see the day when he'd be proud of them. Now he's laying in there, dying, and he knows they don't give a damn. That's pretty hard for a man to swallow."

Mace was silent for a moment, his eyes following Lang as he walked back and forth. Then the sheriff said, "Reckon it would serve them right if Ira cut them off without a dime."

"He won't though, because he drew up his will a long time ago when his wife was living, back when he still figured there was a chance the boys would turn out different. He's talked about changing that will a dozen times, but he never got around to it."

"And now it's too late." Mace removed the pipe from his

mouth and stared thoughtfully at the teeth marks on the stem. He wondered again where he was going to find some help, and then it came to him that he hadn't hit Andy up.

Not wanting to miss any bets, Mace said, "If you're going to quit here, Andy, maybe you'd like to try your hand at badge-toting. I could get you on as deputy."

Andy shook his head. "I'd go loco having to live in town all the time."

"Shucks, you might get where you like it."

"Not me, Mace. Besides, I've got a little place down on the Brazos all picked out. Born and raised in that country and I've had it in mind for a long time to go back."

"Sure about it, huh?"

Andy nodded slowly.

Mace was about to say something else, but he stopped and stood motionless, watching Kate Perry come out of the house. She paused for a moment on the porch, speaking to Lang, and then came on, walking heavily across the yard toward Mace and Andy.

The two men looked at her, waiting, and then she answered the question that was in both their eyes.

"He's gone."

It was something that Mace Lawson had been expecting, and yet all along he had kept hoping Ira would get well, that somehow the doc would pull him through, and then it would all blow over and everybody could stop worrying. But now Ira was dead and there was no one to hold his sons back.

Mace helped Kate into the rig and then climbed in himself. As they drove out of the yard, he had one last look at Lang's cold face, and Mace realized, more than ever before, that he wasn't man enough to stop the trouble that was coming.

Chapter 11

LEAVING THE VAIL STORE, DAMARON RODE TOward the Meegan place, and he was thinking of Mina, realizing that every time he saw her he liked her more. It wasn't going to be easy to ride away and leave her, but what else could he do?

Take her with you, he thought. She'd go if you asked her, and she's used to traveling, living in hotel rooms. That part of it wouldn't bother her, and it would only be for a couple of

81

years. Then you could buy that ranch and the two of you could live there for the rest of your lives.

He caught himself then, swearing softly. He was thinking like a damned fool. His kind of life was no good for a woman. Wait until you're ready to quit and then come back for her. But two years was a long time to expect a woman to wait.

Overhead the sky was blue, except for a few puffy white clouds. It was hot and Damaron could feel sweat in his armpits. His gaze roved westward and he saw the shadows shift on the mountain slopes. Cattle country, he thought. Good grass and plenty of water. A man could ride a long way and not find any range that beat it.

He came to Halfway Creek and saw a rider leaving the Meegan place. It was Ruth Perry, wearing a fringed riding skirt and a white blouse.

When they met, Damaron said, "Howdy. Have you been to see Rollie?"

She stopped her horse close to his, saying, "It was you that I came to see."

Damaron gave her a sober regard.

"What's the matter with me?" Ruth said, pouting. "Do I look like I might have the plague, or something?"

Damaron grinned. "Now what brought that on?"

"You know what I'm talking about, Blain Damaron. You haven't been to see me once."

Damaron looked at her, still grinning. A breeze was tugging at her blouse, pressing it against her breasts. Her Stetson hung between her shoulders, and her hair, a flaming mass in the sunlight, was disarranged in a way that he found attractive.

"I haven't been getting around much," he said.

She tossed her head. "You haven't been too busy to go to the Vail store."

With a wry expression, Damaron dismounted and led his horse to the edge of the stream. The animal began nuzzling the water and Damaron slapped him affectionately on the neck. When he turned around, Ruth Perry had swung down and was coming toward him, leaving her mount with trailing reins.

"Rollie's been going to see you nearly every day," Damaron said. "So I didn't figure you'd be lonesome."

The willow thickets blocked their view of the house, but Ruth glanced in that direction, and then, facing Damaron again, she said with a touch of impatience, "Rollie Meegan is all right, but he's just a kid."

"He's older than you are."

"In years, maybe."

82

Damaron shook his head, puzzled. "I don't savvy you. What are you looking for, anyway?"

She looked directly at him and said, "A man—a real man, like you."

The tone of her voice sobered him and he was conscious of a faint stirring of excitement. He said, "You'd better wait till you grow up some more."

With her eyes still on him, she said softly, "I'm going to show you that I'm more grown up than you think."

She moved quickly then, flung herself against him and threw her arms around his neck. Damaron put his hands on her shoulders and started to push her away, but the warmth and softness of her was too much to resist. He let her kiss him, felt the heat of her moist lips and for a moment he let desire have its way.

At last Ruth stepped back, breathing heavily. She smiled and said, "Now what do you think?"

He stared at her a moment before answering. Then he said, "I think Kate should have tanned your bottom more often."

Ruth pouted again and said nothing.

Damaron got back on his horse. "You keep fooling around," he said, "and one of these days you'll wish you hadn't."

She didn't answer and she was still standing there when he lifted the reins and rode away. Starting toward the Meegan place, he changed his mind and turned toward town. The restlessness was still working on him and he felt the need of a drink.

Thoughts, dark and troubling, continued to parade through his mind. The way old man Wendell had looked at him this morning and the things Wendell said. Killing gets in a man's blood; it's like a tonic to him.

Hell, it wasn't that way with him, and it never would be, so why should he let it bother him? Why couldn't he shrug it off, the way he had always done the looks and the talk that went on behind his back? The money, that was all he was after. But what about two or three years from now? Could he quit the way he had planned or had he gone too far? The danger and excitement did have a certain amount of appeal.

This damned valley, he thought. The land and the people were working on him, stirring doubts and misgivings in him that he had never known before. You should have ridden on because you were doing all right for yourself. A machine, a man without a conscience. And then you met that kid and you started stirring the ashes of the past.

It was late afternoon when he reached Candelaria. He rode directly to the saloon, left his horse at the rack, and went inside. The men at the card tables gave him the usual apprehensive glances and it was quieter in the room than before he had entered.

Morton Baird, serving a customer at one end of the bar, finished and moved to Damaron.

"What'll it be?"

"Whisky."

Baird started to reach for a bottle, then paused and nodded toward a corner table. "Man over there been asking about you."

Damaron turned and looked. The man at the card table was short and stocky with a sharp face and long sideburns. Damaron went over to him, and stopping beside the table, said, "You want to see me?"

"You Damaron?"

"That's right."

The man stood up and held out his hand. "I'm John Niler. In the mining business up at Silver. I heard you were here. Sit down and we'll have a drink."

Damaron hesitated, looking at Niler's oily face and not liking it. But he had come for a drink and there was a bottle on the table. He pulled out a chair and sat down, waiting until Morton Baird brought him a glass.

Niler poured drinks for both of them before he said, "I heard you were through Silver, but you didn't stop long enough for me to see you."

Damaron tasted his drink and waited.

"Like I said, I'm in the mining business and I'm having a little trouble." Niler raised his glass and smiled over the top of it. "From what I hear, you're good at handling trouble."

"Depends."

Niler took a drink and rubbed his lips together. "Good whisky."

Damaron didn't answer. He studied the man across the table from him, noting the large pores in his skin and the gold that showed in his teeth when he smiled.

"I've got a lot of men working for me," Niler said, setting his glass back on the table. "Most of them have families, wives and kids to look after."

This was the way it usually went, Damaron thought. They gave you a sad story, tried to justify their reason for hiring you instead of coming right out and telling you they had somebody they wanted killed.

"There's a tinhorn hanging around the saloon," Niler went on, "and he's taking my boys for plenty with his sharp dealing. Oh, he's slick about it and nobody's caught him yet, but I know what he's doing."

"A couple of your boys ought to be able to handle him, all right."

"One of them tried it and got a bullet in his belly. This tinhorn carries one of them sleeve guns, and he can get it out in a hurry."

"And you want me to run him out of town?"

Niler nodded. "We've got a marshal, but he's afraid to do anything." He paused and lifted his glass again. "How much will it cost me?"

"Five hundred."

Niler reached for his wallet. "I suppose you want part of it in advance?"

Damaron shook his head. "Pay me when the job's done."

"Can you tend to it right away?"

Damaron looked into his whisky glass, considering it. Then he said, "I'm tied up right now. Be a few days before I can get up there."

"Couldn't come tomorrow?"

"No, I'm afraid not."

"Well, make it as soon as you can." Niler glanced at his watch, finished his drink and stood up. "I'd better get started back. Be looking for you."

Damaron nodded and watched the man turn toward the batwings. He could feel the curious stares of the saloonman and some of his customers, but Damaron ignored them, giving the whisky glass his attention. He didn't have to go hunting work, he thought. There were plenty of men like Niler who would come looking for him.

He didn't like Niler any better after he'd finished talking than before he'd started. Something in the man's eyes. Likely his reasons for wanting to get rid of the gambler were personal. Damaron would ask around, find out a few things on his own, the way he always did.

He swore then, asking himself what difference it made. Why couldn't he take a job like some of the other boys in this business? Do what you were paid to do and let it go at that.

The whisky was warm in his stomach. He took another drink and stared at the empty glass. He knew why he had told Niler he would take the job. It was because he had to prove to himself that he hadn't gone soft.

He started to pour another drink, then changed his mind and set the bottle back on the table. He'd had enough. Drink any more and his head would get fogged up—something he was usually careful about.

He left the table and was starting out when the slatted doors parted and Dirk Stobaugh, shouldering through them, drew up and stood there glaring at Damaron.

For a moment Damaron stared at him, damn sure that he wasn't going to step around Dirk, who was blocking the exit. Flatly, Damaron said, "Get out of the way or I'll walk over you."

Dirk's nostrils flared with temper.

Behind Damaron there was the clatter of poker chips, the scrape of chairs as men moved hastily to get out of the way. Suddenly it was quiet in the room and he and Dirk stood there facing each other.

When Damaron started forward, Dirk hesitated for an instant. Then with a muttered curse, he stepped aside and went on toward the bar, his bootheels striking the floor hard.

Damaron went out and, stopping on the porch to roll a smoke, he thought, Dirk won't keep backing down forever. One of these days he'll tangle with you and when that happens you'd better watch yourself.

He went to the rack and got his horse. Riding down the street, he saw Doc Talbot leave the livery stable and turn toward his office. Damaron watched the medico a moment, then reined his horse over to the walk in front of the sheriff's office. Before he left town he might as well see Mace Lawson and find out what was new.

He was wrapping the reins around the rail when Doc Talbot came up, carrying his black bag.

"Hello, Doc," Damaron said.

The medico nodded and switched the satchel to his other hand. He said, "Have you heard the news?"

Damaron looked at him questioningly.

"I just got back from Long S. Ira Stobaugh is dead."

Damaron glanced toward the sheriff's office. "Does Mace know?"

"Yes, he was out there, brought Kate Perry over."

When Damaron started for the office, Talbot said, "Mace hasn't gotten back yet. He was at the Perry place when I drove by." The medico shook his head. "Mace is likely out there drinking coffee and trying to figure out what he'll do when hell breaks loose."

Talbot walked on and Damaron leaned against the rack

for a moment, pondering the medico's words. Then he went back to his horse and as he reined the animal around, his gaze settled on the saloon. He thought of Dirk and wondered if young Stobaugh had come to town to celebrate the death of his father.

Sam Reebe, the hotel man, came hurrying across the street, calling, "Mr. Damaron!"

Damaron stopped and waited for him.

"I didn't get a chance to see you when you checked out," Reebe said as he drew up beside Damaron's horse. "Just wondering if there was anything wrong?"

"Nothing."

Reebe stood there in the dust, looking up. "I just wanted to make sure there wasn't nothing wrong with the room or the service. I'd appreciate you telling me if there was something you didn't like."

"Everything was fine."

"I'm glad to hear you say that," Reebe said. "And if you're going to stay a while, I could make you a special weekly rate. The room would be considerable cheaper that way."

"Thanks," Damaron said dryly. "But I won't be staying."

He lifted the reins and rode down the street, glancing once more toward the saloon. Dirk Stobaugh had come out and stood now on the porch, his narrowed eyes pinned on Damaron, watching him ride out of town.

Chapter 12

THE NEXT MORNING AFTER BREAKFAST, DAMARON and Rollie Meegan were at the corral when they heard hoofbeats, and a little later four men rode into the yard. They were a tough-looking foursome, led by a big man with a red beard and yellow eyes. That one Damaron recognized as Boon Haxen, the Texas outlaw and killer.

When they came to a halt, Damaron said, "You're a long ways from your stomping grounds, Boon."

A grin lifted one corner of Haxen's hard mouth. "So you beat us here, huh, Damaron?"

"I'm not here for the same reason you are," Damaron said.

Haxen laughed without humor. "You hear that, boys?"

The three men behind Haxen didn't answer.

"You have to climb out of bed mighty early to get anywhere ahead of this Damaron," Haxen said, shifting his weight in the saddle. "The first time we come across one another he was already there and had himself set up, nice and cozy."

Damaron, his cool glance taking in the men behind Haxen, said, "Not the same boys you had with you the last time, Boon."

"You know how it is," Haxen said grinning again. "They come and they go."

"Yeah, I know," Damaron said as he reached for his tobacco sack. "Some of them go to jail and others wind up with lead in their guts. Seems like you're kind of lucky, though."

"Not lucky, Damaron. Smart." Haxen's yellow eyes swung to Rollie Meegan and gave him a brief going over. "Who's your friend, Damaron?"

"The name's Meegan," Rollie said, answering for himself. "This is my outfit."

Haxen sent a contemptuous glance about the yard before he looked at Damaron again. He said, "A ten-cow operator like this couldn't make it worth your while."

"You're here to sign on with Long S," Damaron said. "But I told you I wasn't around for the same reason."

One of the men with Haxen, a squint-eyed fellow with loose lips, spoke for the first time. "We've come a long ways, Boon, and I'm so dry I'm spitting cotton. Let's get on to this town, whatever the name of it is."

"Candelaria," Haxen said without taking his eyes off Damaron. "Real pretty name. Spanish, I guess."

"It means 'candle of the road,'" Rollie said.

Haxen ignored him and spoke to Damaron. "We just stopped here to make sure we're on the right trail."

"Just keep on the way you're heading," Damaron said, "and you won't have any trouble finding the Stobaughs."

Haxen leaned forward, one hand on the horn while he looked speculatively at Damaron. "Before I go, I'd kind of like to know how you stand."

"On my own two feet," Damaron said, smiling thinly.

Haxen scowled. "You know what I'm getting at. There's powder smoke in the air and this Long S is hiring guns, but here you're hanging around a shoestring outfit, acting real friendly with this kid."

"Don't let it worry you, Boon."

"I'm not worried—just curious."

"Wait till you have your powwow with Lang Stobaugh. He'll tell you why I'm here."

"You sound like you don't care much for this Stobaugh."

"I don't."

Haxen took his hand off the horn and straightened slowly. "Then I reckon that puts us on different sides of the fence."

The man with the squint eyes moved his hand closer to his gun, and noticing this, Damaron said flatly, "That yahoo on the buckskin looks like he's itching to throw down on me, Boon. Better tell him to ease up before you're one man short."

"Relax, Whitey," Haxen said without looking at the man. "Can't you see me and Damaron are old sidekicks?"

The man called Whitey didn't answer, but his hand fell away from his gun.

Still cautious, Damaron said, "You're stretching things a little when you talk about us being *amigos.*"

"We worked for the same outfit, didn't we?" Haxen asked.

"For about a week," Damaron said. "Then you killed that deputy sheriff, and the last time I saw you, you were making tracks for parts unknown."

"I didn't go far, and while I was holing up waiting for things to cool off, seems like I remember hearing some talk about you switching sides in that fracas."

"You can hear all kinds of things," Damaron answered.

Haxen regarded him for a moment in silence. Then he said, "If you're figuring on staying awhile, I reckon we'll be seeing each other."

With that he lifted the reins and rode out of the yard, the other three following him.

Rollie Meegan, staring after them, said, "That Haxen looks like the kind that could kill you and laugh while he was doing it."

"He could," Damaron said, his moody gaze on the four riders.

Rollie said bitterly, "What chance are the little outfits going to have fighting Long S when the Stobaughs are hiring men like those four?"

Damaron reached for his tobacco sack before he realized he had a cigarette in his mouth, unlighted. He said, "It's going to be awhile before they start crowding you."

"I'm not so sure," Rollie said, and then, touching his holster, added, "I'd better get to practicing."

"How about those new hinges you said you were going to put on the barn doors?"

"They can wait."

With his back against the corral, Damaron watched the kid set up a tin can and pace off the distance. Rollie went about it with the same grim patience, but Damaron could see no improvement in the way he handled the gun. Looking on, he thought, why don't you come out and tell him he's wasting his time, that he'll never be any good with a gun?

While Rollie was reloading, Miles Wendell rode up from the creek on a sway-backed mare. He reined in and with only a glance at Damaron, spoke to Rollie. "Just came over to tell you we're having a meeting at the Perry place right after supper."

Rollie nodded. "I'll be there."

"I've got to get on over to the Saunders place," Wendell said. "I'll see you this evening."

Damaron's eyes followed the old man as he turned and rode back the way he had come.

The day passed slowly and restlessness was growing in Damaron.

As soon as supper was over, Rollie said, "You want to ride over to the Perry place with me?"

"Might as well," Damaron said.

When they had ridden a short distance, Damaron said, "I've got a job waiting for me up at Silver."

"Then you'll be leaving," Rollie said with a trace of disappointment.

"Man made me a pretty good offer."

Rollie looked off into the gathering darkness. "Ruth's going to hate to see you go."

Damaron looked at him. "Why don't you tell her how you feel about her?"

"Kind of hard for me to say what I'm thinking when I'm around her. Besides, she figures I'm not dry behind the ears."

"Give her time, she'll come around one of these days."

After a thoughtful silence, Rollie said, "I liked her the first day I laid eyes on her, but she was going with Ed, and I wouldn't have come between them, even if I had the chance."

Damaron shook his head. "I don't think that gal knows what she wants."

Rollie moved a little in the saddle, and said, "Maybe I ought to treat her rough. I've heard that works with some women."

"You could try it."

Rollie considered it. "Naw, that's just not my way."

They rode on and when they came to the Perry place,

Wendell and Saunders were already there, standing on the porch along with three other men that Damaron recognized as valley ranchers.

Damaron and Rollie dismounted at the edge of the yard. Rollie, starting toward the house, paused and glanced back. "Coming along?"

"I'll wait here," Damaron said.

Rollie went on to the porch, nodding to the men gathered there. Damaron put his back against a cottonwood and watched them while he twisted up a smoke. He saw Ruth come out of the house. She stood there in the lamplight, speaking to the men and to Rollie, and then when Kate joined the gathering, Ruth left the porch and crossed the yard to where Damaron was standing.

"Hello, Blain."

"Howdy, Ruth."

She stopped beside him and turned to look back at the house. "I was hoping you'd come over," she said.

"I didn't have anything else to do."

She was wearing a light green dress that went well with her red hair, and her face had a freshly scrubbed look. His eyes lingered on her for a moment, but he was thinking of Mina Vail, wondering why he hadn't gone to see her instead of coming here.

A small breeze rustled the leaves of the cottonwood, and Ruth, glancing up, smiled and said, "Remember the time you climbed clear to the top to get my cat?"

"And got all scratched to hell," Damaron said, grinning. "Whatever happened to that old tom?"

"He's still around."

"Supposed he'd be dead by now. Man, that cat could sure kick up a racket."

Ruth was still smiling, her eyes intent on his face.

Damaron's gaze returned to the house and he sobered as he looked at Kate Perry and the others. The men were quiet, giving Kate their attention as she talked to them. Rollie Meegan was leaning against a porch post and now and then Damaron saw the kid turn to glance toward the tree.

"Rollie's all right," Damaron said.

Ruth frowned at him. "I wish you'd stop trying to sell me on somebody else."

"Sometimes a person's got what they're looking for right under their nose, but they can't see it."

Ruth started to say something and then turned her head as the clatter of hoofs reached them. Damaron dropped his cigarette and worked it into the dirt with a toe of his boot while he listened to the sound grow louder. A little later, Lang Stobaugh, followed by Boon Haxen and his men, rode into the yard.

Kate Perry stopped talking and the men around her turned to watch the riders as they came directly across the yard and drew up close to the porch. In the pale moonlight, Damaron could see Lang Stobaugh's face. It was cold and hard.

"I heard you folks were getting together," Stobaugh said, swinging down. "I thought this would be a good chance for me to talk to you while you're all together."

The small ranchers, all except Rollie and old man Wendell, began to move uneasily.

Ruth said with quiet concern, "Who're those men with him?"

"His new crew," Damaron answered without looking at her. "A bunch of hired killers."

Kate Perry walked to the edge of the porch and looked at Lang who was standing at the foot of the steps. Behind Lang, Boon Haxen and his men were still on their horses, none of them moving.

Kate said steadily, "I don't want any trouble here, Lang."

His face didn't soften. "I'm bringing in two thousand head of cattle in a couple of days, and that's just to start with. Before I'm done I'm going to have this valley, one way or the other. So you can sell out to me now, or stay on and make it hard on yourselves."

"If you're offering the rest of us what you did Wade Saunders," Wendell said, "you must think we're soft in the head."

"You all know what I'm willing to pay," Lang said. "Take it or get ready to fight."

Boon Haxen spoke for the first time. "And if I was you all, I'd think twice before I decided on trying to buck him."

Miles Wendell, ignoring the red-bearded Haxen, started down the steps toward Lang. "By God!" the old man cried, his voice quivering with rage, "who do you think you are, anyway?"

"Better cool off, old man," Lang said softly.

Rollie Meegan stepped away from the porch post, moving toward Wendell, and saying, "Take it easy, Miles."

Anger had hold of the old man, Damaron could tell, and he was in no mood to listen to anyone. With a curse, he threw himself at Lang Stobaugh, lashing out with both fists.

But the old man's blows were wild and Lang had no trouble dodging them. Then he set himself and drove his right fist with savage force into Wendell's face. The old man staggered back and fell in the flower bed, his arms and legs waving in the air.

Damaron was already moving away from the tree, leaving the darkness that had hidden him and walking now with the moonlight full upon him. He came in behind the Long S men, and because their attention was on old man Wendell, none of them noticed Damaron until he was close.

Lang Stobaugh, taking his hot eyes off Wendell, swung around in time to get Damaron's fist in his mouth. It was a vicious blow, thrown while Damaron was still moving forward and it dropped Lang on the ground as if he had been kicked by a horse.

The squint-eyed outlaw called Whitey reached for his gun, but Rollie Meegan already had his weapon out and was covering Boon and his men. "Just sit, nice and quiet," Rollie said.

Boon Haxen, showing no fear, grinned and said, "This ought to be good. Let's see what happens."

Damaron stood there in the yard, looking down at Lang Stobaugh who was sitting up now and rubbing his jaw. The stunned expression left his face and hate came into his eyes, grew until it was a bright and wicked flame. Damaron watched him, knowing that Lang would fight this time. He had been careful until now, not wanting to take any chances, but this was something he couldn't walk away from.

"You going to lay there all night?" Damaron asked, quietly, tauntingly.

Stobaugh got up, but he took his time and he didn't lunge in. He came slowly, deliberately toward Damaron, and Damaron remembered those fights Lang used to have at school, how nobody had been able to stand up to him. His body was hard and well-muscled and he was as big a man as Damaron.

They came together and Stobaugh's right fist landing in Damaron's ribs was like the blow from a sledge hammer. But Damaron took it and, holding his ground, ripped through Stobaugh's guard and felt his fist smash against flesh and bone.

Kate Perry and Wade Saunders had helped Miles Wendell to his feet and now the old man was sitting on the edge of the porch, watching the fight in silence. No one said anything, until Ruth, moving over to the steps, cried excitedly, "Give it to him, Blain!"

Damaron kept his eyes on Stobaugh, trying to roll his head and miss the next blow that Stobaugh threw, but Lang's fist caught him on the cheek, breaking the skin and bringing blood. Still Damaron didn't back up. He pounded Stobaugh with both fists, slowly, implacably forcing him to give ground. Damaron's next blow cracked against Lang's jaw, straightening him up, but Damaron was thrown off balance and before he could catch himself, Stobaugh had nailed him with a powerful right.

Damaron went to one knee and while he was in that position, shaking his head to clear it, Stobaugh threw himself forward in a furious attack. He landed on Damaron, forcing him onto his back, and began to rain blows down into Damaron's face.

"Now you've got him," Boon Haxen called. "Pour it on."

The words were hardly out before Damaron gave a heave that sent Lang over his head. They rolled in the dirt, coming close to the horses, and one of the animals shied. On his back now, Stobaugh kicked out with his right leg, trying to catch Damaron with one of his spurs. Damaron ducked and had to duck again to keep the horse from stepping on him. He grabbed Stobaugh's leg and pulled him into the clear and started to fall on him but Stobaugh twisted away and got to his feet.

He tried to catch Damaron with a knee under the chin as Damaron was getting up, but Damaron grabbed his boot with both hands and threw him off balance. While Stobaugh was staggering back and trying to keep from falling, Damaron came to his feet and moved in on him. He hit Stobaugh with a right and a left and he kept hitting him, driving him back across the yard. In trouble now, Stobaugh tried to fight back, tried desperately, but what blows he landed failed to stop Damaron.

Stobaugh went down. He groaned and got to his feet and Damaron let him have it again, the blow popping loud in the silence. This time Stobaugh fell hard and lay there, his chest heaving, his face covered with dirt and blood.

Boon Haxen, his voice heavy with mockery, broke the quiet. "I didn't think you were sucker enough to use your hands on a man, Damaron."

The man's words cooled Damaron's anger and he glanced down at his hands, for the first time giving thought to what he had done. His left hand was hurting a little and skin

94

was missing from the knuckles. He didn't answer Boon, his gaze remaining on Stobaugh while he massaged his fingers and his thoughts ran dark and somber.

At last Lang Stobaugh pulled himself up and walked past Damaron, moving slowly, stiffly toward his horse. He climbed into the saddle and put smoldering eyes on the men on the porch.

"What just happened didn't change a thing, and if any of you think it did, you're making a big mistake."

No one answered him and Lang wheeled his horse and rode out of the yard, followed by Haxen and his men. Watching them, Damaron recalled the tight smile on Haxen's face and he knew that he had proved little or nothing to Lang Stobaugh.

We'll meet again, he thought, and the next time it will be with guns.

Chapter 13

LEAVING RUTH, KATE, AND THE OTHERS STARING after him, Damaron got his horse and rode away from the Perry place. There was blood on his face and he reached for his bandanna, trying to wipe the blood off. His left hand was beginning to swell and he shifted the reins to his right, swearing under his breath.

Once more he had taken a chance on breaking his gun hand, but he had been wanting to hit Lang Stobaugh ever since that day in town, and tonight he'd done it. Now that it was over, he decided it had been a damn fool thing to do. He was letting a personal fight pull him into a bigger one, and that wasn't playing it smart, the way a man had to do if he was going to get anywhere.

He came to the Candelaria River and saw the lamplight in Mina's store. In front of the log building he dismounted and went in, calling her name. When she didn't answer, he went out and walked to the river and along the path where he had walked with her that other night.

He hadn't gone far when he saw her. She was leaning against a huge round boulder, looking out across the river. Then she heard him and she looked around, a smile driving the pensive expression from her face.

"I thought maybe I'd find you here," Damaron said.

He went closer and she stopped smiling when she saw the cut on his cheek.

"What happened?" she asked.

"I tangled with Lang Stobaugh."

"You whipped him?"

"Yes, but it took some doing."

She came close to him, inspecting the cut on his cheek, and Damaron could smell the clean, fresh scent of her hair. He put one hand on her arm, caressing it gently while he looked at her and for the first time admitted to himself that he loved her. He loved her and he wanted her and he needed her.

"We'd better go back to the store and let me tend to that cut," Mina said, and started to step back.

Then she saw the way he was looking at her and she stopped and stood very still. Damaron caught her by the shoulders and pulled her against him, almost roughly. He kissed her long and hard, trying to satisfy a pent-up hunger, forgetting everything except his need for her.

The river flowed on, rushing through the darkness, but neither of them were aware of its sound. Then, still holding her against him, he lifted his head, and said, "I love you, Mina. I want to marry you."

Her arms were around him and she put her head against his chest, smiling as she held him tightly. "I've wanted you to say that since the first day I saw you."

He stroked her hair for a moment and then he said, "We'll go to Silver tomorrow, and be married there."

She looked up at him, frowning. "Silver, the mining camp in the mountains?"

"Yes, I've got a job waiting for me there."

"A gun job?"

"Naturally."

Troubled now, she turned her face away and they were silent for a moment while Damaron stared at her.

"You know what I am," he said. "What's wrong?"

When her face remained averted, Damaron said roughly, "Damn it, answer me."

She looked at him then and her face was serious. "It's not what you are, Damaron. It's what you're asking me to do."

"I don't follow you," he said, puzzled.

Her lips moved, but she hesitated as if she were trying to find the right words. "I don't understand it myself, Damaron."

"Start making sense," he said.

She glanced into the darkness and then her eyes came back to his. "I don't want to leave here, and go back to the kind of life I lived with Howard. A few days here and a few days there. Living in hotel rooms, eating in restaurants."

"You knew all along that was my kind of living and you let me believe it wouldn't make any difference."

Damaron's voice was low and rough, but Mina kept looking at him, and now she said, "At first I didn't think it would make any difference, so long as I was with you."

"Now you've changed your mind."

"This country, Damaron, this river. It grows on you and takes hold and makes you realize that where you've been before was nowhere in comparison. At least that's the way it is with me."

He turned and walked to the edge of the river, angry with her for the first time. Angry because her eyes and her mouth had promised so much, and now she was letting him down.

She came and stood beside him and he turned to look at her, hearing her say, "I made a mistake with a man once, Damaron. I won't do it again, and I know now that love isn't enough to make a marriage work."

He was angry and impatient and he said, "The first day I saw you you started giving me a build-up. You had me believing we were a lot alike, had me thinking that maybe with you it would work."

"It could work, Damaron. There's no reason why it wouldn't if you'd forget about leaving and put your roots in this valley. This is your home; where you started from and where you belong now."

He made an impatient gesture and turned to stare in moody silence out across the river.

"Damaron," she said softly, "don't be angry with me."

He said with quiet stubbornness, "You were putting on an act right from the start, pretending to be something that you aren't."

"You're wrong," she said. "I told you that night at the dance that I'd been waiting, looking for a long time, ever since Howard died. I saw you and I knew you were the right one."

"If that's the case, you'll go with me, make the best of it."

"At first I thought I could do that. I thought that having your love would be enough, that nothing else would matter. Howard was weak, Damaron, unable to make decisions, and

97

he had to have someone to lean on. I had all of that I wanted. Now I want to lean on someone else."

"What's that got to do with going away with me?"

"Because it will mean starting out the way I started with Howard. Drifting can get to be a habit. Do it long enough and you'll never be satisfied staying in one place."

He faced her again, trying to be patient, trying to see her side of it. He said, "A couple of years more—three at the most—that's all I'm asking. The time will pass before you know it, and then I'll spend the rest of my life making you happy."

She regarded him for a silent moment. Then she said, "I was married to a gambler, and you'd think I would have learned to take a chance, but I didn't. I have a feeling that when that time was up, you'd find some excuse why we should go on, a little while longer. I'm afraid, Damaron."

"Afraid of what?"

"That a man who has lived as you will never be content to live as other men. You keep telling yourself you can, but how will it be when the danger is gone, when there's no excitement, nothing but work and sweat and the monotony of ranch life?"

He turned away from her again, looking out across the dark river. Her words were running through his mind, stirring doubts, troubling him. But a long time ago he had picked the trail he would travel and he could not turn back now.

"I love you, Damaron," she said softly, "and I want to marry you."

"But not on my terms?"

"No, I won't let myself do that."

"Then I reckon we're wasting time."

He left her standing there and walked back to the store, angry with himself for becoming involved with her in the first place. He had thought she was different when all along she was pretending, trying to make him fall in love with her before she sprang it on him what she was after.

To hell with her, he thought.

He got his horse and was riding away from the store when he heard a horse coming from the direction of the Perry place. A few minutes later, Ruth Perry rode out of the darkness and reined in beside him.

"I thought I might find you here," she said.

Damaron rode on, saying nothing, and Ruth held her mount beside his.

He looked at her then, scowling, "Why'd you come?"

"I wanted to talk to you."

"About what?"

"Just talk."

Damaron was in no mood for idle conversation. They rode for a while in silence and Ruth kept looking at him, her eyes moving over his face. But Damaron was thinking of Mina, remembering the things she had said.

"You sure showed Lang Stobaugh up," Ruth said. "But I'm afraid he won't let it go at that."

"Not if I know Lang like I think I do," Damaron said soberly.

Ruth said in a low, worried tone, "He'll try to kill you, Blain. I know he will."

"I figure he'll try all right."

She reached out and touched his arm. "Why stay here and give him the chance?"

"That's a good question," Damaron said. "Would you blame me if I pulled out while I'm still all in one piece?"

"Whatever you did would be all right with me, Blain."

He glanced at her and smiled. "Thanks, pardner."

Ruth looked unhappy. "Is that the only way you can think of me?"

When he didn't answer, Ruth glanced back toward the store and said dully, "You're in love with Mina Vail, aren't you?"

"I thought I was, but I asked her to marry me tonight and she turned me down."

"I'd marry you in a minute if I had the chance, Blain, and I'd go away with you, go anywhere you asked me."

Damaron said soberly, "I'm not the man for you. I'm nothing but a hired gunman, a drifter. Some have called me a killer, and maybe they were right."

"It doesn't matter, Blain. We'd get along, have fun and be happy together."

"You're making a lot of loco talk, not knowing what you'd be letting yourself in for."

"All I know is that I want to be with you."

He said patiently, "You've built me up into something big and important, but you've been looking at the moon and dreaming too much. I'm the kind you want to steer clear of, the kind that'll bring you nothing but grief."

"Stop running yourself down."

"I'm just giving it to you straight. Rollie's the kind you ought to tie to—steady and dependable."

"Do you think a girl wants a man that gets red in the face every time she looks at him? I tell you Rollie is nothing but a big, clumsy kid, and as far as I'm concerned he doesn't fill the bill."

"You could try being a little nicer to him and see what happens."

She looked away from him, angry for a time, and Damaron gazed across the dark land, his thoughts returning to Mina. How long would it take him to forget her, to put her from his mind and get back to the way he was before he rode into this valley? A man who knew where he was going and what he wanted. Contented with his way of living—and then he had met her and she had thrown him, got him side-tracked. But not for long. He was back on the right road now and this time he'd stay there.

Bringing his mind back to the present, he spoke to Ruth. "How did the meeting turn out?"

"They're going to stick together and fight the Stobaughs."

"Figured they would," Damaron said, "and they don't stand a Chinaman's chance."

Ruth's mount was so close that her knee brushed his leg. She said, "You don't own any land here, Blain, and you don't owe these people a thing. Why be a fool and stay on when you know what it may get you?"

He said musingly, "There's a job waiting for me at Silver."

"Then go there," she cried. "And if you won't take me with you, I'll wait for you. I'll stay here, waiting and hoping that someday you'll change your mind and send for me."

Damaron was quiet for a moment. Then he said, "You'd better head for home, before Kate starts worrying about you."

"Kate never worries about anything except the ranch."

The note of bitterness in Ruth's voice caused Damaron to stare at her closely. Then she was gone and he reined in for a brief interval, watching her ride toward the Perry place. When she was lost in the darkness, he put his horse in motion again, but Ruth's words were still in his mind.

"Why be a fool and stay on when you know what it will get you?"

The Stobaughs were out to get him, he thought, and with Boon Haxen and his boys to help them, Damaron figured it would take some doing to stay alive.

Chapter 14

WHEN DIRK STOBAUGH GOT HOME FROM TOWN that night, he had just enough whisky in him to make him feel right. He went to the house, looking for Lang, and found Lupe, the old Mexican housekeeper, packing her things.

"Where you think you're going?" Dirk asked.

"To town," she said without glancing up. "I have a job at the hotel, washing dishes."

She didn't like him or Lang either, Dirk knew, and he felt like telling her he'd be glad that he wouldn't have to look at her ugly, dried-up face, but he didn't say it because she was a good cook and he didn't like to think how it would be with him and Lang having to eat in the cookshack along with the crew.

"No sense rushing off just because the old man's gone," Dirk said. "I'll talk to Lang and see what he thinks about paying you a little more money."

"Lupe no care about money."

"That's loco talk," Dirk said, leaning against the door-frame. "The Reebes will work you to death, a lot harder than Lang and me will, and they won't give you nothing for it, either."

The old woman went on working, stuffing some of her belongings into a flour sack. "Lupe no care to live in this house any more. She does not like to be around bad men."

"Aw, to hell with you," Dirk said sullenly.

The old woman still didn't look up from her work.

Incoming horses took Dirk onto the porch and he stood there watching Lang and their new riders pull up at the corral. While they were unsaddling, Dirk drifted over and in the moonlight he could see his brother's face plainly. It was swollen and covered with dirt and blood.

"What the hell happened to you?" Dirk asked.

Lang went on unsaddling, not looking around, saying nothing.

Boon Haxen, removing the gear from his own mount, grinned and said, "Damaron caught him when he wasn't looking."

"Well, I'll be damned," Dirk said. "You licked everybody

101

you ever tangled with, and then you let somebody like Damaron get the best of you."

"Shut up," Lang said sharply. "You run off at the mouth too much."

Dirk stood there, quiet until Lang had taken his gear to the barn and then headed for the house. Staring after him, Dirk said to no one in particular, "I reckon it's up to me to stop Damaron."

Boon Haxen, reaching for the saddle blanket, stopped and laughed without humor.

Dirk gave the red-bearded man a narrow look. "You think I can't do it?"

"I've got my doubts."

"I don't wear this six-shooter just for looks," Dirk said.

The man called Whitey turned his mount into the corral and came back to stand beside Boon Haxen. Whitey said, "A lot of men pack guns that don't know how to use them."

"Not me," Dirk said, putting his shoulders back. "You fellows think you're talking to a runny-nosed kid, you're crazy."

"Listen to him brag," Boon said with a grin.

The others grinned too, showing their amusement, and Dirk glanced at them. "Bragging hell," he said. "I killed a man with this gun a few days ago. Met him in the street and shot it out with him."

"Fair and square, huh?" Whitey said.

Dirk nodded. "Right out in the open where everybody could see it, and this fellow wasn't any greenhorn, neither."

Haxen was still grinning. "Wait till you've put lead in as many as I have and then you can talk."

Dirk sneered. "How many you killed?"

"Twelve."

Dirk blinked and his mouth came open a little.

"And that ain't counting a few Indians," Haxen said.

Dirk simmered down. He said, "Rufe Ketchell said you were a good man; that's why we sent for you."

"Too bad about old Rufe getting his tail in a crack," Haxen said. "But he never was too bright; that's why I had to let him go."

"He's in Canon City now," Dirk said. "And I reckon he'll be there for quite a spell."

"That's what happens," Haxen said, "when you go off half-cocked."

Whitey started toward the bunkhouse, saying, "Let's play some poker."

Dirk watched them walk away, four men who were as tough as they came. He had tried to impress them with his big talk, but he knew they didn't think much of him. Haxen had grinned when Dirk had mentioned getting Damaron, as if he figured a boy shouldn't be starting out to do a man's job.

Resentment stirred in Dirk and he swore aloud as he went into the corral and cut out a mount. While he was saddling he could hear Haxen and the others laughing and talking in the bunkhouse.

Riding out of the yard, Dirk built up in his mind how it would be if he were to kill Damaron. He could picture the looks on Haxen's and that Whitey's faces. They wouldn't grin at him any more and he bet they'd be pretty careful how they talked. Dirk had been trying to convince himself that maybe he was good enough to take Damaron on, but now with the effects of the whisky wearing off, he wasn't so sure.

Damaron was fast. A man had to be to build that kind of reputation. The thought of meeting him face to face brought the sweat out on Dirk and he could almost feel lead tearing into his guts.

He rode toward the Meegan place and his thoughts turned to the old man and he remembered how he had stood there at the burying, feeling nothing, while old Lupe carried on and stayed there at the grave for a long time after everybody else left. All Dirk could think about was that the old man wouldn't be able to use that strap on him any more, and that now he was on his own. He could go where he wanted to, do what he damned pleased and there was nobody to stop him.

He came to the Candelaria and rode along the river until he reached the Vail store.

Pulling in on a brush-covered rise, Dirk sat his saddle and looked at the lighted doorway of the store building. He thought of Mina and remembered what Ketchell had said about the ones that had been married being the best.

Dirk leaned forward, one hand on the horn. There was a horse in front of the store which meant Mina wasn't alone. Then, while Dirk looked on, Damaron came up from the river and, seeing him, Dirk reined his mount back into the brush. Out of sight, he watched Damaron go to his horse and ride off.

A little later Mina came out of the darkness and went into the store, but Dirk's eyes followed Damaron. Before he had gone far, Damaron was joined by Ruth Perry, and Dirk, watching them ride along through the moonlight, thought, with grudging admiration, he's got both of them women after him.

When Ruth and Damaron were out of sight, Dirk looked at the store again, thinking of Mina, telling himself she was alone now. He had been to the store before and she had never been very friendly toward him, but that didn't bother Dirk. Ketchell had told him a lot about women, said that most of them liked to play hard to get.

Always before when he was here, Dirk had to watch himself and not get out of line, but that was because he was afraid of what he would get from the old man. Now he didn't have to worry.

Riding toward the store, Dirk remembered what Lang had told him about staying away from the women. Dirk stopped his horse, undecided for a moment, and then he thought, hell, he ain't telling me what I can do.

He rode on across the yard and as he drew up, Mina appeared in the doorway. Dirk smiled at her and said, "Evening."

Mina didn't return his smile. She said coolly, "I'm closed for the night."

She stood there with the lamplight behind her and Dirk looked her up and down, excitement growing in him even though he couldn't see anything.

"You're not acting very neighborly," Dirk said, still sitting his saddle. "Long S is going to have this whole valley before long, and we could throw you a lot of business."

Mina stood there, watching him carefully, and now she said, "There's some business I can do without."

"Pretty high and mighty, ain't you?" Dirk sneered. "Maybe you think that with Damaron around you don't have to worry about nothing."

"I didn't worry before Damaron came."

"Think he's something, don't you?" Dirk said, sneering again. "Well, I wouldn't get my hopes up too high if I was you because Ruth Perry was waiting for him when he rode away from here a little while ago, and the last I saw of them they were hitting it off real nice."

"I'll be open at six in the morning," Mina said.

When she started to step back and close the door, Dirk said, "Now I wouldn't do that if I was you because if you do I'll just have to kick it in."

Mina left the door open and moved back into the store.

Dirk smiled to himself, figuring he had put the fear in her. He'd go in and show her it didn't pay to fool with a man like him. He slid out of the saddle and was almost to the doorway when Mina appeared again in the opening. This time there was a gun in her hand, and the sight of it caused Dirk to halt abruptly.

"Get back on your horse," Mina said sharply.

Dirk hesitated. He looked to see if she were bluffing, and could tell by the set of her face that she wasn't.

"Pulling a gun on me, huh?" he said sulkily. "I'll remember this."

"You better remember something else," Mina said, and the gun was steady in her hand. "You come around here again and I'll kill you."

Dirk got back on his horse and with the reins lifted, he said, "One of these days I'll take some of the fire out of you."

He wheeled his horse then and rode away from the store, going in the direction Damaron had gone. If Mina thought she had scared him into staying away, she had another think coming. Couldn't see him because of that Damaron. Seemed like everything he did, Damaron was there to get in his way.

Kill him, Dirk thought, and then you'll be top dog. Ruth and Mina wouldn't be so hard to get. Hell, he bet he'd have all the women after him. But how could he manage it? Wait in the brush somewhere with a rifle—but bushwhacking Damaron wouldn't get Dirk what he wanted. He'd have to get close enough to use a short gun and it couldn't be in the back, either. Must be some way he could work it so folks wouldn't know.

Keeping to the shadows, Dirk rode toward the Meegan place and he got to thinking how it would be if he could take Damaron into town, face down across his horse. He'd say, "There's the great Damaron. He wasn't so much. I killed him, Me, Dirk Stobaugh."

That made pleasant thinking and Dirk got carried away. Other gunmen like Boon Haxen would stay out of his way, remembering that he was the man who had downed Damaron. Hell, maybe he'd go away for a while, drift around the country like Damaron had done, and see the sights. His reputation would get him anything he wanted.

First he'd have to help Lang get the valley, because he knew his brother wanted it more than anything. Owning a

105

lot of land might be all right for Lang, but Dirk couldn't get very worked up over the thought of it.

He came to the Meegan place, approaching it slowly, warily. Then he got down and, leaving his horse in the willow thickets along the creek, he moved through the brush until he came to the edge of it. From here he had a good view of the house and in the moonlight he could see Damaron sitting on the steps, smoking a cigarette.

Dirk grinned, thinking that a man did get a break once in a while. It was too far to nail Damaron from here, but if he went down apiece and worked his way in behind the house he shouldn't have any trouble at all. There was no light in the house which meant that Rollie was likely asleep.

Dirk stayed there a moment longer, staring at Damaron's shadowy shape. Looked like he was doing some deep thinking, sitting there all by himself. Just sit there a little longer, Dirk thought as he turned back into the brush. That's all I ask.

He moved through the darkness, putting his boots down carefully. Then he cut away from the creek, the darkness concealing him as he slipped past the barn and went on to the rear of the house. He stopped and stood there for a minute, his gun in his hand. He had to play it right. One little slip, one little sound, and he'd never have another chance like this. He began to work his way toward the front of the house and the butt of his gun turned wet from his sweating hand. After a few steps he drew up to listen again, but there was no sound anywhere, only the hard beating of his heart against his ribs.

There was moonlight at the front of the house, but here at the side you couldn't see a damned thing. He had to feel his way along, but in another minute he'd reach the corner. Then he'd jump out and when Damaron turned to look at him, Dirk would cut him down.

Then Dirk had reached the corner of the house. He peered out cautiously, ready to make his leap. He could see the steps, but Damaron wasn't on them. Now where the hell had he gone, Dirk wondered, and then he stiffened as he caught a sound behind him. He started to whirl, but something hard jammed into his back and Damaron's voice said, "You'd better drop it."

Dirk dropped it, figuring he was dead if he didn't.

"I ought to kill you," Damaron said. "I ought to put a bullet in your belly and watch you kick awhile."

When Dirk didn't answer, Damaron prodded him with the gun barrel. "Get on out in the light."

Dirk walked to the front of the house just as Rollie Meegan, drawn evidently by the sound of Damaron's voice, came onto the porch in his nightshirt.

"What is it, Blain?" Rollie asked.

"Dirk Stobaugh," Damaron said as he put Dirk's gun in the front of his shirt. "Just caught him sneaking up on me."

"I was still awake," Rollie said. "But I didn't hear a thing."

"After a while," Damaron said, "you get where you can hear a fly scrape his feet. Heard something when he reached the back of the house, so I went around the other way and came in behind him."

"All right," Dirk said. "So you caught me. Now what are you going to do?"

Damaron was thoughtful for a moment. Then he said, "I'll turn you over to Mace Lawson."

Dirk's confidence came back. It was his word against Damaron's, so if he went to jail, he wouldn't be there long. He looked at Damaron, thinking, I'll get another chance, and next time I won't muff it.

Chapter 15

IT WAS LATE WHEN DAMARON REACHED CANdelaria with his prisoner. Most of the buildings were dark and there was no one on the street. They left their mounts in front of the sheriff's office and went inside, Damaron walking behind Dirk, his gun in his hand.

A lamp in a wall bracket had been turned low, its dim light showing Damaron the cot against the wall on which Mace Lawson was sleeping. The sheriff, lying on his back, was snoring loudly and his weight caused the cot to sag almost to the floor.

"Wake up, Mace," Damaron said, and had to call again before the lawman stopped snoring and opened his eyes.

"Snap out of it," Damaron said. "I brought you some business."

Lawson sat up, rubbing his eyes with the backs of his hands. He looked at Damaron and then at Dirk Stobaugh.

"What's he done now?" Lawson asked wearily.

Damaron explained while Lawson sat there rubbing the back of his neck.

When Damaron finished, Dirk, who had been silent until now, said sullenly, "I went over there looking for a Long S stray. That's all."

"Sure you did," Damaron said.

Lawson said uneasily, "Well, he didn't take a shot at you or nothing."

"No, but he was fixing to."

"Can you prove that?" Dirk asked.

Lawson went over and turned the lamp up. He fooled with the wick, taking longer than was necessary. Damaron watched him and then turned to look at Dirk. There was a small, mocking smile beginning to form on Dirk's mouth.

Moving away from the lamp, Lawson shook his head, and said, "I don't know what to do about this."

"There's only one thing to do," Damaron said, and he was still holding his gun in his hand. "Lock him up."

The sheriff rubbed the back of his neck again, and seemed to have trouble meeting Damaron's gaze.

"We ought to have a witness," Lawson said. "Did Meegan see anything?"

"Rollie was in bed," Damaron said with growing impatience. "I told you how it was. Isn't my word good enough?"

"To me it is, but the law says—"

"You've got enough to hold him on," Damaron cut in. "Stop stalling, Mace, and put him in a cell."

Lawson was sweating. He walked over to the desk and picked up the key ring. He said heavily, "I don't figure it'll do much good. As soon as Lang hears about it he'll have a lawyer down here."

Dirk stood there, smiling.

"I should have put a bullet in you while I had the chance," Damaron said. "Then we wouldn't have to be doing all this wrangling."

Lawson glanced toward the cell block. "Come on, Dirk."

"I can stand some shut-eye, anyway," Dirk said.

When they had gone down the corridor, Damaron put his gun away and crossed to a window. He stood there looking out at the dark street, asking himself again why he had let Dirk live when he knew Dirk would try again to kill him as soon as he was out of jail.

Lawson came back presently and tossed the key ring on the desk. He sighed and said, "I don't see why you brought him here. Why didn't you kill him and have it over with?"

Damaron walked toward the water cooler in the corner,

saying, "It would have been easier on you that way. Is that what you mean?"

"I've got enough to worry about without having Lang jump me over this deal."

Damaron had a drink and turned around, wiping the back of his hand across his mouth. He asked, "What are you afraid of, Mace?"

"Of dying, I guess, the same as most folks."

"Just thinking of yourself, huh?"

"Isn't that what everybody does?"

"I reckon it is," Damaron said.

"If you don't look out for yourself," Lawson said, "nobody else will. I found that out a long time ago."

Damaron started for the door. "I'll see you tomorrow."

Lawson was sitting on the cot, staring at the floor when Damaron went out.

He had told Rollie before leaving that since it was so late he would spend the night in town. He rode to the livery, put his horse in a stall, and went out without rousing Harry Stiles who was sleeping in his cubbyhole office.

At the hotel, he got Sam Reebe out of bed, and the man came to the door, grumbling until he saw who it was.

"Mr. Damaron," he said, smiling. "Good to have you back."

"Just want a room for the night," Damaron told him. "Tell me which one and you can go on back to bed."

Reebe looked disappointed. "I thought maybe you'd decided to take a room by the week."

"The one I had empty?"

"Yes, we haven't rented it since you left. But I'd better get you some fresh water and see if there's towels."

"Never mind," Damaron said. He left Reebe standing there, got the key off the board, and went upstairs.

The room was hot, still holding the day's heat, and as Damaron undressed he remembered the cool nights at the Meegan place. He got in bed and lay there staring into the darkness, thinking of the meeting at the Perry place and his fight with Lang. He wondered if in whipping Lang in front of the small ranchers he had only served in bringing them trouble that much sooner. Lang might not wait long now.

Damaron rolled over, trying to find a more comfortable position, and then his thoughts turned to Mina and it was a long time before he could put her from his mind and go to sleep.

The next morning he had an early breakfast and left the

hotel dining room. Walking toward the livery stable he passed the hardware store where Jess Hines was busy sweeping the porch.

"Morning, Jess," Damaron said.

"Morning, Blain."

Damaron started on and then swung back, saying, "I could use a box of shells."

Hines nodded and leaned the broom against the front of the store. He went inside and Damaron followed and stood at the counter while Hines waited on him.

"That the gun I sold you?" Hines asked when he had laid the box of shells on the counter.

"Same one," Damaron said, reaching for the box. He opened it and began filling the empty loops in his belt.

"Always felt kind of guilty about letting you have it," Hines said. "You were just a kid and I've wondered a hundred times, I'll bet, if I did the right thing letting you have it."

"Like I told you, Jess, I would have got it, one way or the other."

"I know, but it's bothered me just the same, caused me to think that if I hadn't had the gun in the window maybe you wouldn't have been tempted."

Damaron shook his head. "Keeping things out of sight don't do any good, Jess. Whisky, cards, women, guns—it's all the same. They're here and we've got to learn to live with them."

"I don't know," Hines said dubiously. "We're not all built alike. Something that you can take or leave alone maybe gets to eating on another fellow. As long as it's out in the open he sees it and he keeps thinking about it, but maybe if those things were covered up so he couldn't see them all the time—"

"It wouldn't make any difference, Jess. A man knows what's in this world, and trying to hide the bad things from him won't keep him from wanting them, and getting them if he sets his mind to it."

"Maybe you're right," Hines said, picking up the money that Damaron laid on the counter. "There's lots of things I wonder about. Sometimes I lay awake half the night, thinking, trying to figure it out."

Damaron smiled. "You'll never find all the answers, Jess, so you might as well stop trying."

He went out and walked to the livery stable. When he was leaving the barn on his way out of town, he saw Boon Haxen and his three men making the turn onto Main Street.

110

Instantly wary, Damaron watched them come toward him, and he could see the smile on Haxen's bearded face.

"So, you're still around, huh?" Haxen said when they met.

Damaron, watching him and the men behind him, said, "Does it bother you, Boon?"

"Nothing much bothers me. It's just that I had a hunch that after what happened last night you'd be kissing this burg good-bye."

"If I decide to pull out, Boon, it'll be because I'm damned good and ready, and the Stobaughs or you or those three yahoos riding with you won't have anything to do with it."

The man called Whitey cursed and his squint eyes were full of malice as he said, "This bird's starting to rub me the wrong way, Boon."

Haxen was still smiling. "You've got to watch that temper, Whitey, or it'll get you killed, sure as shooting. Too early in the day to be kicking up a ruckus and besides, we come to town to do some drinking. Let's get at it."

Damaron held the reins in his left hand, his right hand in the clear and ready to reach for his gun if necessary. The one called Whitey was itching to have a try at him, but Haxen was giving the orders, and, looking into the big man's yellow eyes, Damaron thought, if it comes to a showdown, you'll have all of them on you.

He rode on out of town, telling himself he'd go to the Meegan place and get his warsack. There was no use hanging around any longer. He'd shown Rollie all he could, and besides he had that job waiting for him at Silver. With Dirk in jail, Lang would hold off a while, so now was the time to pull out.

He looked across the valley, green and bright in the morning sunlight, and he liked the smell of the grass. Maybe when his time was up and he had his stake he'd come back. Maybe Mina would still be here, but if she was, she'd be married to somebody else. A woman like that wasn't going to sit around waiting for a man that might never get back.

He didn't like the trend of his thoughts, so he started contemplating the job that was waiting for him at Silver. That wouldn't take long and after that where would he go? Cheyenne, maybe, but what the hell difference did it make? Hang around the mining camp a while and wait for somebody to hire you. You won't have to wait long. You never do.

He came to a rise overlooking the Meegan place, and drew up for a minute, gazing down at it. A good outfit, and if the kid got the breaks, he'd make out all right here. He looked at the corral and the barn and as his eyes settled on the house, he saw Rollie come out, carrying a pail.

Damaron lifted the reins and rode down the slope. When he reached the yard, Rollie was drawing a bucket of water from the well. He finished pulling it up and then turned, watching as Damaron dismounted.

"You get Dirk to jail all right last night?" Rollie asked.

Damaron nodded. "Lawson had him in a cell when I left."

Rollie lifted the bucket, saying, "Without you here, I wasn't able to make a dent in the coffee pot this morning."

"I'll have a cup with you now."

They went to the house, Rollie carrying the bucket of water, Damaron beside him. Somehow he hated to tell the kid he was leaving, but his mind was made up and there was no use dragging it out. When he had poured himself a cup of coffee, he stood beside the stove sipping it.

"You still figure on taking that job at Silver?" Rollie asked without looking at him.

"Yeah," Damaron said. "I just came out after my warsack."

"Been good having you here. I don't know what I'd have done after Ed was killed if you hadn't been around."

"You'd have made out."

"No, I'd likely have got myself killed trying to square things for Ed right off the bat, and I'm much obliged for the gun savvy you've passed along to me."

Damaron held the coffee cup, watching the steam drift up from it. He said soberly, "I showed you all I could, kid. The rest is up to you, but I can tell you something for sure."

Rollie looked at him questioningly.

"You've got a long ways to go before you're good enough to take Dirk Stobaugh on."

"Yeah, I guess I have."

Damaron drained the cup and turned away from the stove. He got his warbag. There was an odd feeling inside him as he gathered up a few belongings. With the warsack on his shoulder, he took one last look at the room and went out with Rollie following him.

"If I ever come through here again," Damaron said, smiling, "I expect to find you and Ruth Perry married and raising a batch of kids."

When Rollie didn't answer, Damaron said, "You keep working on her."

Rollie nodded and he was trying to smile.

Damaron stepped into the saddle and lifted the reins. "So long, kid."

"So long, Damaron."

He rode to the edge of the yard and glanced back. Rollie was still standing there, a forlorn figure in the sunlight. Damaron lifted his hand and rode on.

Chapter 16

ROLLIE MEEGAN STOOD THERE IN THE YARD, watching Damaron until he was of sight, and there was a heaviness inside the kid. Not until now had he realized how much he had come to depend on Damaron, how much he had come to like him during his short stay at the outfit.

Walking toward the barn, Rollie remembered the fight last night, and the envy he had felt when he'd seen Ruth looking at Damaron, admiring him. He guessed that was what all women wanted, a man who knew how to take care of himself, fight if need be.

In no mood to stay on the outfit, Rollie saddled up and rode toward the Wendell place. He'd find out if any of the other ranchers had heard from Lang Stobaugh since the meeting last night. When he came in sight of the Wendell ranch, he saw old Miles come out of the corral, take one look in his direction, and run for the house.

A moment later the old man reappeared with a rifle in his hands. He was bringing it up when Rollie hollered at him. Recognizing Rollie then, Wendell leaned the carbine against the front of the house and came into the yard.

"Had me worried there for a minute," Rollie said, pulling up close to him.

"After last night I'm not taking any chances on them Stobaughs or some of their gunhawks slipping up on me."

Rollie stayed on his horse looking down at the old man. He asked, "How's the jaw feel?"

"Not as bad as Lang's I'll bet," Wendell said with a grin. "Reckon it'll be quite a spell before he forgets that beating."

"Ready to admit you were wrong about Damaron?"

Wendell was thoughtful for a moment. "I don't know what to make of him. Figured he was like all the rest of his kind, but now I'm not sure."

Rollie said wistfully, "I wish I was half the man Damaron is."

"What happened to him?"

"He's pulling out, going up to Silver."

Wendell looked searchingly at Rollie and said, "The way you two seemed to be hitting it off, I thought maybe you'd go with him when he left."

Rollie shook his head. "Everything I want is right here in this valley."

"Don't know how long we can last against the Stobaughs," Wendell said. "And I've got a hunch that Wade Saunders and some of the others might be hard to hold when Lang starts putting on the pressure."

Rollie glanced out across the range. "I think I'll ride over and see how Wade's making out."

"You hear anything, let me know."

Rollie nodded and turned toward the Candelaria River. Old Miles, he thought, would be the only one who could do much good when the showdown came, and Rollie had a feeling it was coming soon. Revenge had been all he could think of for a while, but last night at the meeting it had come to him that he was one of these people now. They were his friends and neighbors and their troubles were his.

He came in sight of Mina Vail's store, and he thought of Damaron again. Sure would have been fine if things had worked out between him and Mina, but from the way Damaron had acted last night, he and Mina had squabbled about something.

When Damaron was leaving this morning, Rollie had considered offering him a partnership in the ranch in the hopes of getting him to stay. But Rollie hadn't said anything because he knew that Damaron wouldn't be interested in a deal like that.

Rollie rode up to the store, frowning when he saw a wagon in the yard. Wade Saunders was sitting on the high seat, his wife and one of the children beside him. The other two youngsters were seated on a mattress that had been tied on top of a lot of other household belongings.

Wade Saunders, holding the lines loosely in his big hands while he talked to Mina Vail, turned to look at Rollie.

"What you fixing to do?" Rollie asked, eyeing the loaded wagon.

"Pulling out," Saunders said bitterly. "Getting out and letting the Stobaughs have the outfit."

Rollie glanced at Mina and saw the troubled lines in her face as she stood there beside the wagon looking up at the Saunders.

"I thought we had it settled at the meeting last night," Rollie said. "Agreed we'd all stick together."

114

"That was last night," Saunders said. "But I got to milling it over, and I figure it's just plain stupid trying to buck Lang Stobaugh. It's my outfit he's going to hit first, and I've got a family to think about."

Rollie said patiently, "You don't have to be in a rush, Wade. Dirk's in jail so wait a few days and see what happens."

Saunders shook his head stubbornly. "Those killers Lang hired aren't in jail, and I'm not going to stick around waiting for them to pay me a visit."

Mrs. Saunders, her face pale and drawn, said, "We have to think of the children."

Saunders spoke to the team, and Mina, stepping back from the wagon, said, "Why don't you stop in town and stay there until the trouble is settled?"

"Maybe I will," Saunders said. "But I don't see much sense of it."

Rollie sat his horse and he and Mina watched the Saunders wagon pull away, neither of them saying anything for a time. Then Rollie, looking at her, said quietly, "I guess Damaron told you he was leaving?"

Something came and went in the woman's eyes, and she murmured, "Yes, I knew he was going."

Rollie glanced in the direction of the Perry place, saying, "Reckon I'd better get over and let Kate know about the Saunders pulling out."

"Be careful, Rollie."

He nodded and rode away from the store. When he glanced back she was still standing there staring after him. Make some man a fine wife, Rollie thought, but he guessed there was no woman that could hold Damaron.

When he reached the Perry place, Kate was at the corral saddling a horse.

"Just going to town," Kate told him.

Rollie glanced toward the house and saw Ruth's face at the kitchen window. The sight of her made him ill at ease and he returned his attention to Kate.

"Thought you'd want to know that Wade Saunders has decided not to stay."

"He can't do that," Kate said, swearing softly. "As soon as the others hear about it they'll be ready to tuck their tails too."

"I tried to talk him out of it," Rollie said, "but he wouldn't listen."

Kate finished tightening the cinch and swung aboard. "May-

115

be I can talk some sense into him. Which way was he heading?"

"Toward town," Rollie said, glancing toward the house again. "You want me to go along?"

"I'll handle it," Kate said, and rode away from the corral, sitting the saddle and handling the horse as well as any man Rollie had ever seen. He stared after her for a moment and then looked again at the kitchen window. The curtain was back in place.

He rode around the house and, leaving his horse in the shade of a cottonwood, went to the back porch. The rattle of dishes ceased and Ruth came to the door, a dish towel in her hand.

"Hello, Rollie," she said without interest.

"Just thought I'd talk to you a few minutes," he said, feeling awkward and uncomfortable in her presence the way he always did. "Can't stay long."

Ruth held the door open for him and then went back to the wood range.

"Coffee?" she asked.

"No, thanks," Rollie said, holding his hat and twisting the brim. "Not now."

Ruth was wearing a red and white checked apron over her dress and her hair was pinned up, piled high atop her head. It reminded Rollie of a red sunset. He stood beside the table, watching her work, wanting to tell her how he felt, but not knowing how to go about it.

"Your mother's gone to try to talk Wade Saunders out of leaving," he said.

Ruth was drying a plate, her back to him. She said, "What we need is a man like Damaron."

Rollie knew she was right, but he felt that twinge of envy. He ran a finger around the sweatband of his Stetson, saying, "Damaron's leaving."

"Why shouldn't he? This isn't his fight."

"I don't blame him for going," Rollie said, shuffling his feet. He paused and then spoke again. "I reckon you'll miss him plenty?"

As if she were talking to herself, Ruth said, "I asked him to take me with him, but he turned me down."

Rollie looked at her, remembering those nights he had come here to visit, but she couldn't see him the way he wanted her to. She never would if he didn't do something about it. Now was the time to tell her. Put it off and he might

116

wind up with one of the Stobaughs' bullets in him. The way it was going he stood a good chance.

When she came to the table with a stack of dishes he watched her put them down and as she started to turn away, he said, "Ruth."

She stopped and looked at him, waiting.

"Ruth, I've got to tell you something."

When he hesitated, she said, "Well, what is it?"

He could feel the heat in his face and his throat was dry, but he couldn't stop now. Suddenly he blurted, "Ruth, I—I love you. I want to marry you."

She stared at him, her lips parted in surprise, and then she threw her head back and laughed, a low, mocking sound. Rollie wanted to crawl through the floor, but as she continued to laugh, he began to get mad. His anger grew until abruptly he reached out and grabbed her, not realizing what he was doing. He jerked her up against him, and holding her with one hand used the other to force her head back.

"Rollie Meegan, you—you—"

The words were drowned out as his mouth came down on hers. He held her hard against him and kissed her, his lips bruising and demanding. Then he let her go and without waiting for her reaction, he swept past her and stalked out of the kitchen.

He got his horse and rode toward Candelaria town with Ruth's laughter still in his ears. He'd tried to show her he wasn't any kid, but now, with the anger draining out of him, he realized it took more than a kiss to prove you were a man.

When he wasn't far from town, he saw Kate Perry riding back and there was a slump to her shoulders that told him she hadn't been able to talk Saunders out of leaving. Rollie cut through a stand of timber, not wanting to talk with Kate after what had happened with Ruth.

She was in love with Damaron, or thought she was, and she'd never be convinced Rollie was a man till he proved it to her. He rode on and came to the outskirts of town. Ahead of him he could see the Saunders wagon, rattling along, the two kids still sitting on top of the load.

The wagon made the turn onto Main Street and was out of sight for a moment. When Rollie reached the bend in the road and could see the wagon again, six riders were coming down the center of the street, leaving town. He recognized Lang and Dirk and thought with a swift rush of bitterness, Lawson has let him loose.

117

Boon Haxen and his men were with the Stobaughs and as the six men passed the Saunders wagon, Dirk looked at it and laughed. The wagon kept moving and the Stobaughs came on toward Rollie Meegan. There was time for him to pull off the street and cut down an alley and avoid meeting them, but the kid was in a reckless mood now and he thought, I could have it out with them right here. Kill Lang and Dirk and the others won't stick around.

The distance between them narrowed and he could feel their hard stares. His eyes settled on Dirk and he remembered that day he had ridden into town in time to see Ed Colby die, shot down by a man that would go on killing because everybody was afraid of him.

The riders were close now and then they stopped and Dirk Stobaugh, mean and tough and resentful, said, "Now where the hell do you think you're going?"

"Nowhere," Rollie said and was surprised that he could stay as calm as he was. In a minute he'd be dead because as soon as he reached for his gun, they'd all cut loose. They'd kill him for sure, but not before he got Lang and Dirk.

"Look at him," Dirk said with a sneer. "Packing a gun and trying to act real big."

"To hell with this," Lang said sharply. "Let's get on."

Dirk, ignoring his brother, said, "Hold on a minute. I want to find out what this yahoo's got on his mind."

"You want to know," Rollie said softly. "I'll tell you. It's this!"

He reached for his gun, finding out what it was like to face something besides a tin can. He saw the cold smile on Dirk's face, the eagerness that flared in his eyes, and then, while Rollie was still trying to get his gun out of the holster, Dirk's gun tipped up and he said from the corner of his mouth, "He's my meat."

Lang Stobaugh, looking on with stony indifference until now, spurred his horse forward, knocking Dirk's gun down with a chopping blow as he went past. Rollie had his gun free, but before he could fire, Lang was on him, driving his horse against Rollie's mount. While the kid was off balance, Lang whipped out his gun and brought the barrel down against the side of Rollie's head.

Dazed, but still conscious, the kid fell out of the saddle. He hit the ground and lay there, struggling to rise. As though from a long way off, he heard Lang's voice.

"Dirk, you kill-crazy damned fool. I just bailed you out of jail, and now you're trying to get back in."

"Lawson's not going to lock me up again, and if you think I'm going to set here and let that bastard pull a gun on me you're crazy."

Stunned, Rollie lay there, shaking his head, and then he discovered he still had the gun in his hand. He tried to lift it, but Lang, swinging down, kicked the weapon away from him. Then he swept the street with his brooding gaze, and said to his brother, "If you want to do something, work him over."

"I ain't busting my hands up," Dirk growled.

"He didn't say anything about using your hands," Boon Haxen said, grinning. "If you don't know how to pistol-whip a man, I'll give you a demonstration."

"You ain't stealing this show," Dirk said as he dismounted. "Stand back and give me room."

Rollie Meegan had staggered to his feet. He stood there, swaying, his mouth open, trying to focus his eyes on Dirk Stobaugh. All he saw was a fuzzy shape coming toward him. Rollie tried to back away, but Dirk lunged forward, his gun barrel shining in the sunlight. There was pain, sharp and hot as the gun barrel landed, laying his cheek open. He tried to break away, but Dirk stayed close to him and hit him again and again. Each time the barrel landed, skin ripped and blood spurted.

Rollie fell and pulled himself up and struck out blindly, trying to get his hands on Dirk. Once he succeeded, but Dirk cursed and clubbed him with the gun barrel across the bridge of his nose and the hold was broken. Darkness reached for him and he reeled through it, came up against a horse. He heard a man laugh and a boot jabbed him in the back, kicked him into the open.

He stumbled forward and Dirk was waiting for him. The gun barrel raked back and forth across his face and he went to his knees. In that position he remained a moment while blood ran down his face and into the dirt. Then he got up again, using the last of his strength, and Dirk, careful until now not to hit him too hard, let go with a vicious blow to the side of his head.

Rollie went down on his face and the darkness rolled over him.

Chapter 17

STOPPING AT THE SALOON ON HIS WAY OUT OF town, Damaron was having a last drink when Mace Lawson came in and moved up beside him.

"Dirk's out of jail," the sheriff said dismally. "Lang came in and raised so much hell that I had to let him go."

Damaron put his glass down and regarded Lawson with disgust.

Lawson said defensively, "I couldn't rightly hold him without you staying to appear against him at the trial."

Damaron picked up his glass and drained it. "To hell with it," he said roughly. "I'm not sticking around for a deal like that."

Baird, the saloonman, came up, and Lawson ordered a beer. When the mug was in front of him, he began to turn it slowly on the bar. Without looking at Damaron, he said, "So you're pulling out today?"

"Yeah," Damaron said, and he was thinking of Mina. "I've stuck around here too damn long already."

"A lot's happened since you came to town."

When Damaron didn't answer, Lawson lifted the mug and took a sip of beer. He frowned, tasted the beer again, and made a face.

Morton Baird, standing a short distance down the bar, was watching Lawson, and now the saloonman asked, "What's wrong with it?"

"I don't know," Lawson said, giving the mug a critical stare. "Don't taste right."

"Same beer I've been serving all along." Baird came over and lifted the mug to inspect it. "You want me to draw you another one?"

"I'm out of the notion now," Lawson said. "Forget it."

"Have a drink of whisky," Damaron said, nodding toward the bottle in front of him.

Lawson shook his head. "Too early in the day for me to be drinking hard likker."

Damaron shrugged and poured one for himself. Watching him, the sheriff smiled dimly and said, "The day you rode in here, I got my hopes up, thinking maybe I could talk you into taking a deputy's job. When you turned me down, I went

120

to Kate Perry and got her to work on you, figuring that since you knew Kate pretty well, maybe she could turn the trick."

Damaron looked at the shot glass, saying nothing.

"I've been around this town for a long time," Lawson went on. "Seen a lot of them come and go. Your dad, for instance. Never could beat him playing checkers." The sheriff sighed and wagged his head. "I've had it mighty easy, drawing pay for sitting on my rump, and I've drifted along that way, satisfied and knowing that when election time rolled around I had enough friends to keep me in office."

Damaron rolled the glass between his fingers, telling himself he should be on his way. If he left now he could make it to Silver before dark and he wouldn't have to hurry. And the way Lawson was wound up, he'd likely talk all day.

"Man gets used to a good thing and when he sees he's about to lose it, he gets desperate. At least that's the way it was with me. All that talk I gave you about getting on the right side was just talk and nothing else. I was thinking of myself instead of Kate and the other ranchers, and of what I stood to lose when the Stobaughs let loose."

Damaron cut him an oblique glance. "Why the hell are you telling me all of this?"

Lawson's shoulders lifted and fell. "Just need to talk to somebody, I reckon, and get it off my chest."

"You've done a lot of talking, but you haven't said much."

Lawson was leaning against the bar, one foot on the brass rail. He shoved his hat back a little and said, "Down there at the jail a while ago when Lang come and told me I'd better let Dirk out, it hit me—something I'd been trying to dodge all along."

"What?"

The sheriff looked across the room, staring at nothing. "I'm a fourflusher, fat and lazy, and looking for somebody else to do my job for me. I've hit up everybody and his brother, trying to unload my responsibilities on them. That's not right, Damaron. A man's got to hoe his own row; he can't expect others to do it for him."

Damaron laid some money on the bar and glanced toward the street. "I'd better get started."

"Good seeing you again, Blain, and I hope everything works out like you got it planned. And I want you to know that I don't blame you none for not taking the job and maybe getting your ears shot off for a bunch of folks that don't mean nothing to you."

"So long, Mace."

Damaron left him standing there and turned toward the slatted doors. Before he reached them they swung open and Jess Hines rushed in, calling to the sheriff, "Mace, get out here!"

"What's up, Jess?" Lawson asked, starting across the room.

"It's Rollie Meegan. I think the Stobaughs killed him."

Damaron went out, his searching glance sweeping the street. Townsfolk were moving along its length, hurrying toward the far end of town. Without waiting for the sheriff, Damaron got on his horse and rode to where the crowd was gathering. He swung down and when the people saw him they fell back to let him through.

Rollie lay there, blood from his battered face wetting the dirt. Damaron reached him and knelt down, feeling for a heartbeat, speaking to Angelo, the barber, "How'd it happen?"

The little Italian shook his head. "I justa got here."

Damaron lifted Rollie and carried him down the street toward the doctor's office. Mace Lawson and Jess Hines fell in beside him.

The sheriff asked in a tight, strained tone, "Is he still alive?"

Damaron nodded and kept walking.

"Hold up a minute," Lawson said. "Let us give you a hand."

"It's not far now," Damaron said. "I can manage."

He went on, carrying that dead weight in his arms, and the crowd came behind him. When they reached Doc Talbot's office, the medico was on the porch. He held the door open, saying, "Put him on the cot."

Mace Lawson and Jess Hines came into the office, both silent until Damaron had laid Rollie down. Then Hines said, "I saw it from the porch of my store. God, it was awful, but I was too scared to do anything."

"Which one of them did it?" Damaron asked.

"Dirk. Rollie tried to pull his gun on them." Hines shook his head. "Can you imagine that crazy kid standing up to the Stobaughs and their hired killers."

"Beats me," Lawson said.

The doctor was bending over Rollie, working on his face, and Hines watched for a moment without saying anything. Then he said, "Rollie had his gun out, but Lang jumped him before he could get off a shot. And then Dirk went to work on him with a gun."

Damaron stood there, wrath gathering and spreading through him.

The doctor, still busy, said without looking up, "I think he's coming to."

Rollie stirred, half lifted his right leg, and then a groan came from his split lips.

"Easy, son," Doc Talbot said gently.

Rollie lifted his head and then let it fall back. He groaned again and his half-opened eyes went to Hines, moved to Lawson, and came to rest on Damaron. He said in a whisper, "Figured you were gone."

Damaron's throat felt tight and a sense of guilt was troubling him.

"Lie still," Talbot said. "I'll have to take some stitches."

Rollie winced and said bitterly, "I tried, but I couldn't get the job done."

Damaron didn't hear Mace Lawson leave the office, but when he glanced around the sheriff was gone. Jess Hines had sat down on a stool. He looked as if he were going to be sick any minute.

"The doc will fix you up, kid," Damaron said quietly. "I'll see you later."

"Where you going?" young Meegan asked.

Damaron was already turning toward the door. He didn't stop, but he said, "To finish what you started," and went on out of the office.

He got his horse and was riding out of town when he saw Mace Lawson walking slowly, heavily, toward his office. He won't go after them, Damaron thought, he's afraid.

Damaron rode on, hitting a steady pace across the valley toward Long S. The job waiting for him at Silver was forgotten and all he could think of now was Rollie Meegan, a kid whose face would be scarred for life. A kid who was slow with a gun—and yet he had tried to stop the Stobaughs.

A breeze touched his hot face, causing him to glance at the sky. It was dark and cloudy. Looked as if it might rain before long. In the west the San Juan Mountains made a somber, uneven line. His gaze came back to the trail and once more he was conscious of that deep and disturbing sense of guilt.

He came to the Perry place and stopped when he saw Ruth on the porch.

"I thought you had left, Blain."

"I got detained," Damaron said. "Rollie jumped the Stobaughs, and they worked him over with a gun barrel."

"Is he hurt bad?" Ruth asked with quick concern.

Damaron nodded and looked past the girl as the door opened and Kate stepped onto the porch.

"What's this about Rollie?" Kate asked.

"He tackled the Stobaughs all by himself," Damaron said. "He's at the doc's office in pretty bad shape."

"I'm going to him," Ruth said, and left the porch, running toward the corral.

Kate stood there with searching eyes on Damaron. "And where are you headed?"

"To Long S," he said, and rode out of the yard.

"Blain, you damned fool," she called after him. "Alone, you won't stand a chance against that bunch."

He didn't answer her, didn't even glance back, and as he rode toward Long S the smell of rain was in the air. He remembered the day he had ridden into the valley on the trail of a killer and he thought of all that had happened since then. A lot had taken place in a short space of time.

In the late afternoon he reached Long S headquarters and drew rein on a ridge overlooking the buildings. Leaving his horse, he walked a short distance. Cedars grew thick here and with the trees to conceal him he scanned the yard below. He saw a man come from the barn and walk toward the bunkhouse where he paused a moment to glance at the sky before going inside.

There was fury in Damaron, but there was also caution. It was the Stobaughs he wanted, but he wasn't fooling himself that he could take them on as long as Boon Haxen and his men were there to back them. The only thing to do was wait until it was dark and he was sure that Lang and Dirk were at the house by themselves.

A drop of rain splatted against the back of his hand and thunder made a low rumble overhead. He went to his horse and got his slicker. By the time he had slipped it on the rain was coming down. He swore softly, not liking the thought of waiting here in the wet. Then it occurred to him that the rain might keep the Stobaughs home and give him a better chance to slip up on them.

After supper, Boon and his men would likely go to the bunkhouse and start a card game. That was what he was counting on. The realization that the Stobaughs' hired killers would come on the run as soon as the shooting started didn't change Damaron's mind. He'd have time to face the Stobaughs, and after that it didn't matter.

With grim patience he waited there on the ridge while the rain fell around him, turning the dirt to mud. Water ran

124

from the brim of his hat and rattled on his slicker. He didn't know how long it was before he saw the men go to the cookshack. Just a little longer now, he told himself and took his gun out, protecting it with his slicker while he checked the loads. The same gun that had taken him from this valley and seven years later had brought him back.

He waited, his eyes on the cookshack, and there was nothing to do but think and wonder about the trail he was traveling. His gaze strayed toward the Candelaria River and he thought of Mina and he remembered words she had said at that last meeting.

It was almost dark now, and then he saw them come out of the cookshack, six men, four of them hurrying toward the bunkhouse, the other two turning toward the ranchhouse.

Damaron waited until the yard was empty and then went back to his horse. He mounted and rode down from the ridge, the rain in his face. He pulled his hat lower and went on, planning to circle the house and come in from the rear. From the direction of Candelaria town came the sound of hoofs, faint but growing louder.

Damaron changed his course and rode away from the ranchhouse, wanting to intercept those oncoming riders before the sound of their travel attracted the Stobaughs. He rode over a rise and drew up, unable to see the riders through the rain and darkness. But they were close now and he waited on the trail until they reached him.

There were three of them, Kate Perry, Mace Lawson, and old Miles Wendell. Two men and a woman who had pushed their horses hard, Damaron could tell. He looked at them, his eyes narrowed against the rain.

"After you left my place," Kate said, "I went to get Mace. We ran into Miles on our way back. There was no time to round up any more."

The sheriff's slicker was tight across his belly. He said, "I was looking for a hole to crawl in, but Kate told me if I didn't come she was coming alone."

Damaron looked soberly at Kate Perry. "This is no place for you."

The woman wiped water from her ruddy face and said, "I can handle a gun as good as any man that ever came along."

She would stay, Damaron knew, in spite of anything he could say. He glanced back toward the Long S headquarters and was thoughtful for a moment. Then he said, "Boon Haxen and his men are in the bunkhouse. You three give me time

125

to make it to the back of the house and then cut loose and keep shooting so they don't get out."

Miles Wendell nodded. "We can keep moving and they won't know how many they're up against."

When Damaron started to turn his horse, Mace Lawson said, "Hold on a minute."

Damaron stopped and looked questioningly at the fat man. Lawson dug under his slicker and tossed a shiny object to Damaron. He caught it and saw that it was a badge.

"Might as well make it legal while you're at it," Lawson said.

Damaron dropped the badge into the pocket of his slicker and rode into the rain-washed darkness. Kate Perry, Wendell, and Lawson came behind him. When he glanced back they were dismounting at the edge of the yard, drawing their rifles and moving into position.

He skirted the yard and pulled up under a tree in back of the house. Before he had time to dismount, one of the three across from the bunkhouse fired, sooner than Damaron had counted on. There was the sound of shattering glass, followed by a startled yelp. Then three rifles were laying down a steady fire.

Damaron was moving across the yard when the back door of the house opened and Dirk Stobaugh came out with a gun in his hand. He started for the corner of the house, stopped and whirled when he saw Damaron coming toward him. Damaron's gun was out. He waited until Dirk got off a quick shot, and then pulled the trigger of his own pistol. The bullet smashed into Dirk's chest and drove him back against the house. He dropped his gun in the mud and, bending to pick it up, fell on his face.

A bullet tugged at Damaron's slicker and he turned to face the back door. Lang Stobaugh had come onto the porch, but at the sight of Damaron, Lang halted. He fired and when he saw that he had missed, he began to move back. He reached the door, and Damaron, walking toward him through the rain, sent a bullet into the doorframe close to Lang's head.

Stobaugh cursed and ducked back inside.

Damaron stepped away from the opening as Stobaugh's gun roared again. He made it to the end of the porch, stepped upon it, and began working his way toward the door. Lightning flashed, and then it was dark again. Damaron moved along the wall, slowly, cautiously toward the door. When he reached it, he stopped and listened. There was the sound of rifle fire and he knew that Kate and the others were keeping

Boon Haxen and his men busy. Caught by surprise, Boon was probably trying to decide whether to make a break or sit tight.

Inside the house a floor board squeaked; the sound told Damaron that Lang was moving toward the front part of the house. Damaron slipped through the doorway and drew up, listening again. Evidently the Stobaughs had put out the lamps when the shooting started, for the house was dark now.

Damaron started across the room and came up against a table. He moved around it and went on. He found a door that opened onto a hall. In the opening he paused, knowing that Stobaugh was waiting for him somewhere in the darkness not too far away.

Starting along the hall, Damaron drew up, for lightning was flashing again. In the brief flare of light, he saw Lang Stobaugh at the front door. The door was open and Lang was ready to step out.

"This way, Lang," Damaron called.

Stobaugh spun around fast and his gun hammered. The bullet screamed past Damaron's head, but he stood still and fired at the muzzle flash. His first shot missed, but the second one caught Stobaugh and slammed him through the doorway and across the porch. He fell down the steps and lay at the bottom of them.

The hard beat of hoofs reached Damaron, telling him that Boon Haxen and his men had made a break for it. By the time he reached the porch, three men were pounding away from the corral, firing wildly into the darkness. Someone yelled and Damaron saw one of the gunmen fall from his saddle. The other two milled for a moment, then spurred their horses out of the yard.

Damaron knelt beside Lang Stobaugh long enough to see that he was dead, and went on across the yard. The man lying near the corral was Boon Haxen. The red-bearded gunman was sitting in the mud, holding his shoulder, when Damaron reached him.

"It's all over, Boon," Damaron told him. "The Stobaughs are both dead."

Haxen cursed. "By God, we were setting in there waiting for the rain to stop and all at once somebody started shooting. We couldn't see nothing and we didn't know what to do."

A moment later Kate Perry, Mace Lawson, and Miles Wendell rode across the yard. Boon Haxen, still holding his

127

shoulder, looked at them and scowled. "You mean there was just three of you out there? And one a woman at that!"

"That's all," Lawson said.

"You all right, Blain?" Kate asked.

Damaron nodded. "Only two got away, so there must be another one in the bunkhouse."

"Yeah, Whitey," Haxen said sourly. "One of you nailed him through the window."

Damaron moved over to Mace Lawson and handed him the badge. "I'll give this back to you now, Mace."

"Sure you don't want to keep it?"

Damaron shook his head. "It's not for me, Mace. I'm going to be a rancher."

Kate Perry looked at him and she was smiling.

Damaron got his horse and rode toward the Candelaria River. It was still raining when he reached the Vail store. He went in and stopped and stood there with water dripping off his slicker. Mina was working behind the counter. When she saw him she stood very still for a moment and then she came out from behind the counter and walked toward him. She moved slowly at first and then increased her pace and came into his arms with a small cry.

"I'll get you all wet," he said.

"Who cares," she whispered. "You're back. You didn't go away."

"I never will," he said. "I'm here to stay."

She lifted her head and he looked at her, knowing that a gun could never buy him what he saw in her eyes.